MURDER

IN A

SOMERSET

VILLAGE

Utterly addictive cozy mystery fiction

JON HARRIS

THE BOOK FOLKS

Published by The Book Folks

London, 2023

ISBN 978-1-80462-130-1

www.thebookfolks.com

MURDER IN A SOMERSET VILLAGE is the second novel in this addictive series of cozy English mysteries. Head to the back of this book for details about the first, MURDER ON A COUNTRY LANE.

For Eli

Chapter 1

Julia stood in the cold, echoey space of the garden centre and stifled a yawn as Mark examined the display of paint cans in great detail.

The sedate pace of village life trundled on and Julia's only worry was the amount of painting that lay in her future, little suspecting that her friend already lay dead.

Her boyfriend tore his eyes briefly away from the paint selection and looked at her questioningly. "Something the matter?" he asked.

Julia forced herself to hold back a catty reply about watching paint dry. Owning a bookshop was, after all, her dream, even if he'd been keen to see it happen, and he'd already sunk large amounts of money and effort into renovating the old library, far beyond what she could ever reasonably have asked of him.

She managed a smile instead. "No, all fine," she said.

Mark returned the smile and then picked up two cans of paint which, as far as Julia could tell, were completely identical, and held them side by side, comparing them. Dating a painter had its pros and cons. A wistful sigh escaped Julia's lips but luckily Mark didn't notice.

"Pass me one of the quick-dry ones, would you?" Mark asked, indicating them with a nod of his shaved head but without removing his eyes from the paint.

Julia reached for the paint, stretching as high as she could, but her fingertips only grazed the bottom of the tin.

"I can't reach," she said.

Mark placed one of the tins he was holding back on the shelf and looked over. "Sorry, I forgot you were short," he said.

"I'm not short, I'm *petite*," Julia said curtly.

"That's just French for short," Mark said.

Julia didn't know if that was true or not, so she left Mark to examine his paint.

From immediately behind Julia's shoulder, a song boomed out and she gave a little start, her slight frame jumping. For the third time since they'd been there, the face-height TV screen launched into its advert for wood varnish, the brightly dressed presenter loudly extolling its virtues and value. Julia found something in their fixed smile and unblinking glare disturbing. Perhaps she was just in a bad mood.

The presenter's performance was interrupted by the sound of Julia's own singing as her phone went off, filling the hall with a personalized ringtone of her serenading her fur baby, Rumpkin, with *Who Let the Dogs Out*, the animal in question yapping furiously out of time in the background.

Wandering a few paces away so she could hear over the advert, Julia pulled her phone from her coat pocket. A photo of Sally was lighting up the call screen. Sally was her friend and sometimes colleague. Julia hoped she was calling in the first capacity.

"Hi, Sally," Julia said, thumbing the answer button and cutting the song mercifully short.

"Hi, chicken," Sally's voice replied. "How are you?"

"All good, thanks. What's up?"

Sally's voice was as sweet as one of her pies when she replied. "Oh, nothing much. Ivan was wondering if you could cover a waitressing shift tomorrow. Barry didn't show up today and we've been absolutely slammed."

Well, it seemed she was calling in the second capacity.

"I really need to give Mark a hand painting the shop. He's already doing so much. Anyway, maybe Barry will show tomorrow?"

"I'm not sure Ivan would take him even if he did," Sally said. "He was furious with him. Said that he'd never let Barry darken the Barley Mow's doors again."

Julia bit her lip. Not that she'd blame the landlord for finally throwing in the towel with Barry. The number of times he'd shown up late or missed shifts altogether beggared belief.

"Please," Sally implored.

"Fine," Julia said. "I'll square it with Mark, but I expect he can cope without me."

"Thanks, thanks so much. Maybe on my day off I can pop in and help with the painting."

Julia had heard that one before. Besides, she still had terrible, terrible memories from when the two of them had painted the living room and she wasn't entirely sure it was a bad thing if Sally stayed away.

Julia made her way back to Mark, finding him still looking at the same two paint cans. "Problem?" he asked, not looking up.

"Sally called. Apparently, Barry hasn't been showing up to work again. She wanted to know if I could cover his shift tomorrow."

"Yeah, fine," Mark replied.

"Really? I thought you'd be mad," Julia said.

Mark shrugged. "It's not ideal. We've still got plenty of time to get the shop sorted, though. And the extra money might help."

Julia peered at the price tag on the paint cans and silently agreed.

With that, Mark deposited both cans of paint into the already heavily laden trolley and began hauling it behind him, past a stack of discounted goods that hadn't managed to sell over Christmas, in the direction of the exit.

"You know, Barry only lives round the corner from here," Julia said. "We could call in on the way home and see if I can actually talk some sense into him."

"Good plan," Mark agreed.

* * *

The rain had slackened to a drizzle that danced in the van's headlights. Julia hated this time of year. The dark evenings and the freezing cold dog walks. And to make it even more miserable, dead Christmas trees lay discarded in front of houses, waiting to be collected.

She was so wrapped up in sombre contemplation of them that she almost missed the turning for Barry's house.

"Here," she said suddenly, pointing across the road.

With impressive reserve, Mark eased the brakes on just in time to turn off the road towards the spacious driveway.

As he did so, a little white Micra came shooting out, its headlamps still off, and swerved onto the road with an audible squeal of rubber.

Mark swore and pumped the brakes, harder this time, sending both him and Julia roughly forward into the grasp of their seat belts. The car behind Mark gave an angry hoot at the Micra as it veered over the central line before disappearing out of sight around the bend.

Mark gave a few more choice expletives as he guided the van steadily up the driveway and then came to a halt. He glanced over at Julia. "Are you okay?" he asked.

Julia just nodded a reply. After a couple of traumatic experiences with cars in the months prior she'd become easily unsettled in traffic. She found driving nerve-racking and constantly tried to hit a phantom brake pedal when she was a passenger. "Yes," she said eventually, as her heart rate settled down. "I'm sure the drivers are getting worse around here, though."

"You might be right," Mark said. He nodded towards the house. Twin rows of ankle-height outdoor lights picked out the path to the front door. "I'll wait in the van, if that's all right?"

"Sure," Julia said, unbuckling herself and stepping down into the spitting raindrops. As she swung the door of the van closed, she heard the muffled sound of Radio 5 Live as Mark switched the radio on.

Julia hurried up the brick paving towards the house. It was a large, detached place set far enough back from the main road that it was shielded from the worst of the traffic noise. Barry didn't live in the main house, but in the small annex that had been built about twenty years ago for some now-departed relative of the owners. Julia had only been once or twice before, sent at Ivan's behest to collect Barry when he'd been late for work.

She went up to the door for the annex and pressed the little circular light of the doorbell, hearing it go off inside the building. There was no cover so she hiked her collar up against the falling rain as she waited.

When there was no answer, she pressed the bell again. She was about to give up but glancing to her side she could see daggers of light shining out from between the slats of the blind and pounded loudly on the door. As her fist landed, the door, evidently unlocked, swung open on its hinges. Barry's modest kitchenette stood behind the now-open doorway, but there was no one there.

"Barry?" Julia called, hearing her voice echoing back at her.

Keeping her toe just outside the threshold, she leaned her body through the door to see round into the kitchenette and called again, louder. "Barry?"

The word subsided in her throat and she gave a scream, backing away from the door and covering her face with her hands, trying to unsee the grisly sight that she had just been confronted with.

Her frame shook with sobs as she kept her eyes screwed tightly shut, oblivious to Mark rushing towards her until he put his arms around her.

"What is it?" he asked. "What's the matter?"

She opened her eyes to see Mark's angular face contorted with worry for her.

At first she couldn't get the words out. She forced away the images of Barry lying on his kitchen floor in a pool of blood.

"It's Barry," she finally managed. "He's dead."

"Dead?" Mark asked, eyes widening. "Are you sure?"

Julia nodded.

"I'd better call Dad," Mark said.

Chapter 2

Blue lights flashed aggressively, a ghoulish counterpoint to the pixie lamps lining the path.

The paramedics were already finishing up, there was little enough they'd been able to do for Barry. But the work of the police was just beginning. A knife in the back could only mean one thing.

Mark's dad, Detective Inspector Rhys Jones, re-emerged from the annex and back out onto the rain-slicked block paving of the driveway. The rain had stopped although the air was still damp and chill. Despite this, he didn't wear any overcoat, his rather amorphous frame covered only in one of the ill-fitting dark suits that he favoured when he was at work.

He made his way over to where Julia and Mark stood at the edge of the property, doing their best to be out of the way, his heavy black shoes making no effort to avoid the puddles as he strode in a straight line towards them.

The inspector distractedly wiped through the white bristles of his moustache with the back of one of his index fingers and cleared his throat, a surprisingly sonorous procedure that took no small amount of time.

"Yes, well," Jones said in his gentle Welsh lilt, apparently replying to a question that no one had asked. "A rather nasty business all this. Very nasty indeed, in fact."

Neither Julia or Mark said anything, so Jones cleared his throat once more, produced a small, black notebook from his inside jacket pocket and smartly clicked the top of a pen. "And I gather you were friends with the deceased, Julia?" he asked. He was evidently trying to make himself sound gentle and understanding, but it didn't quite work with his naturally gruff bearing.

Julia wiped her eyes, already puffy and red from crying and gave a sniff. "I've known Barry since school," she said. "He was a couple of years above me, though. And we worked together occasionally at the Barley Mow. We weren't close, exactly. But I was fond of him. In a way."

"In a way?" Jones asked, one eyebrow raising.

"I mean he was quite infuriating. Lazy, argumentative. But he went out of his way to find Rumpkin on the day he ran off, and wouldn't even take credit for it. That meant a lot to me." Julia shook her head. "Who could have done something like this?"

Inspector Jones let the question hang in the cold air.

"Maybe it was a robbery gone wrong?" Mark suggested.

His dad sucked the air in through his teeth. "No sign of forced entry," he said. "If the deceased let his killer into the house, then chances are it was someone he knew."

Julia and Mark exchanged an uneasy glance.

Julia gave a small shudder. It was hard to think that anyone in such an unassuming and sleepy place as Biddle Rhyne would be harbouring that level of ill will that they could go into someone's home, take a knife and… Julia cut the thought short.

"Well," Jones said, looking down at the scrawl in his notebook. "It looks like the owners of the main house aren't home so we're unlikely to get anything there, unfortunately. And the neighbours are all a bit far off to have seen or heard much, but I'll get the uniforms to ask them just in case. When did the two of you last see Barry?"

"Last night," Julia said, and Mark nodded his agreement. "We were working late painting the bookshop and he stuck his head in after he finished his shift."

Jones wrote this down. "Did he want anything?"

"I think he was just killing, I mean, I think he was just wasting time while he waited for the bus."

"Okay," Jones said. "Now, you say that you saw a car speeding away as you arrived. A white Micra."

"That's right," Mark replied.

"Any chance it belonged to the main house here?" Jones asked.

"Not very likely," Julia said.

Mark looked up at the rather grand structure of the main house. "Agreed," he said. "It was rather a beat-up old thing."

Jones nodded as he scribbled away at his pad. "I'll check anyway. You didn't happen to notice the licence plates, did you, either of you?"

Julia and Mark both shook their heads. "Sorry."

"It would have been a bit of luck," Jones said.

"We could keep an eye out for it around the village," Julia offered helpfully.

"Sure, that would be helpful," Jones said.

Julia could tell he was fighting to keep the condescension out of his voice and gave a sideways glance at his son.

Mark gave a little shrug. "An old, white Nissan Micra. There will be ten of them in the garden centre car park on any given day. Without the plates it's a tough ask."

Julia took their point, but she mentally resolved to keep a look out for it anyway. After all, if she hadn't taken it upon herself to investigate after Mrs White was murdered in the village last year, Jones would never have caught her killer.

"Well," Jones said. "I think that's that. I know where to find you if I need anything more."

The inspector gave a rueful smile but Julia was in no mood at all for levity and didn't return it.

Jones flipped his pad shut with a loud snap and pushed it back into the pocket where it had come from. "I'm sure you'll be wanting to get home."

"Thanks, Dad," Mark said and turned to Julia. "Come on, let's get you back. Do you want me to stay with you tonight?"

"That's fine," Julia said as they made their way towards the van. "I've got Sally and Rumpkin at home. That's plenty."

* * *

As Mark's van pulled away up the quiet, residential street, Julia made her way up the driveway towards the front door, squeezing past the weathered paint of Sally's car to get there.

It wasn't late, only about half nine, but Julia felt like she could collapse into bed and sleep for a whole day, she was so tired.

She let herself into the house, the door opening straight into the living room at the foot of the stairs, flicking the hall lights on as she entered.

Either hearing the door slam, or noticing the light in the hall, Sally appeared at the top of the stairs and raced down. Her blonde curls were tied back pragmatically and she was wearing a plain, fitted black outfit that suggested she had only recently returned from work at the pub.

Julia also noted that she was wearing a solemn, worried expression on her normally bubbly and cheerful face.

"I take it you've already heard, then," Julia said as she took her coat off and added it to the pile under the stairs.

Sally arrived down on the ground floor and enveloped her friend and housemate in a warm hug. "News travels fast in Biddle Rhyne. You know that," Sally said, still holding her tightly.

Eventually Julia managed to wriggle her slender frame free and could sense Sally looking her up and down.

"How are you, chicken?" Sally asked.

Julia did her best to smile, but it didn't go well. "You know…" she said. "And how are you? You knew him better than I do." Or did, she mentally corrected herself. Sally was only a year below Barry in school and the two of them had worked together at the Barley Mow far more than she had, since she only covered the odd shift.

Sally waved the question away. "Yes, but finding him like that? It must have been just awful."

Julia couldn't deny it so she made a non-committal noise, padded past the sofa and cast herself down into the armchair, dislodging the book that she rarely found time to read nowadays.

In front of her, the gas fire by the bookshelves was burning away, the warmth spilling out of it. Rumpkin lay on his side directly in front of it, toasting his belly. At first appearance he might be taken to be asleep, but Julia was wise to this and could see one eye, glinting slightly in the firelight, regarding her lazily.

"Come here." Julia clicked her fingers at the animal. She saw an ear twitch but she hadn't elicited any further movement. She snapped her fingers again and repeated the command. "Come here."

The terrier loved her, she knew, but apparently he loved the gas fire more. With a protesting wheeze, Rumpkin stirred himself and rose to his feet, loping across the few feet of carpet to Julia and finally clambering into his mistress's lap where she gave him some rough but affectionate patting.

"I love you," Julia told the dog.

Rumpkin gave a woof in reply which Julia chose to interpret as 'I love you, too'.

Sally watched the scene unfolding. "I'm just going to set this washing and then I'll come back and we can talk," she said, plucking at the hem of her work shirt.

"Yeah, throw mine in, too, would you?" Julia asked, craning her head back over her shoulder at Sally. "I don't think it ever made the wash from my last shift."

Sally scrunched her face up. "No one's expecting you to have to work tomorrow," she said. "Even Ivan isn't that much of a taskmaster, you know?"

Julia shrugged. "No, that's fine. I want to. I don't want to mope about here by myself with my thoughts. And if I have to look at another can of paint I might actually scream. I could do with the distraction of the pub. Mark will understand."

Sally hesitated a bit before answering. "If you're sure," she said.

"I am."

"Well," Sally said. "Ivan will be happy to see you at least. We're doubling up the lunch services now, so it's all hands to the deck."

"Doubling them up, why?" Julia asked. But Sally had disappeared into the kitchen and not long afterwards came the noise of the washing machine spinning. It came gently at first, but soon shuddered into a powerful rattle that shook the whole house. With a little luck Sally would remember to take the shirts out to dry before the morning.

Julia pulled Rumpkin closer and squished down into the chair. She shut her eyes but despite her tiredness sleep wouldn't come. She could only think of poor Barry. The inspector said it was probably someone he knew, but who could have wanted to hurt him like that? Ivan wasn't fond of him and neither were most of the staff at the pub, but not to the extent they'd do something as horrible as that.

There was one other name that Julia could think of who might have held a grudge against Barry. But she couldn't honestly believe they'd have it in them to harm him. She'd have to go and speak to them.

Chapter 3

The village of Biddle Rhyne, such as it was, was soon left behind in the rear-view mirror as the car headed down the pitted surface of the empty country lane, its worn tyres occasionally finding a pothole or loose stone and sending a vibration up through the vehicle.

Julia looked out of the passenger window. On the other side of the deep drainage rhyne, the fields stretched away into moorland. Some of the rhynes around the moors were little more than ruts for the water to run into. But some, like the one running alongside the lane, were a good four feet deep, probably closer to five after all the rain they'd had this winter. A few careless drivers had discovered the hard way just how deep they could be. Once, a few years ago now, someone had even killed themselves by throwing themselves into one of the rhynes at the other end of the village. Julia had always been rather wary of them after that. At any rate, she felt that Sally drove far too close to them.

The sun was weak and grey, little more than a smudge on the horizon. In this anaemic light the landscape looked forlorn and gloomy. A few cows plodded along despondently, their hooves sinking into the slush of mud. One of them put its head back and lowed. Even they seemed miserable today.

As they rounded the corner, the Barley Mow appeared from behind the hedging that ran along the other side of the road. The colourful sign of the pub's namesake was barely visible in the overcast sky since the spotlights were not turned on, but deep, warm light spilled from roughly shaped windows that punctuated the whitewashed walls of the sprawling old coaching inn.

Sally continued over the gravel to the side car park leaving the choicer parking spots for the patrons, came to a halt and ratcheted the handbrake on.

Julia squinted through the mud-flecked windscreen in confusion. "What on earth's going on?" she asked.

A few hundred yards away, down at the end of the pub's beer garden, a pair of small diggers were hard at work, their mechanical arms hauling great scoops of mud out of the ground. The last time Julia was here, only a few days before, there had been a swing set there – a decrepit, completely unused and probably marginally unsafe swing set, admittedly, but a swing set nonetheless – and it was a surprise to see the twisted metal frame cast aside in a crumpled heap next to the low wooden boundary fence.

"Oh, yes, they started on that a couple of days ago," Sally said, turning off the engine and pulling the driving gloves from her hands – the short drive from their house was nowhere near long enough for the car to warm up properly. "With everything that went on, I guess that it slipped my mind."

"What slipped your mind, exactly? What are they up to?" Julia asked, as the two women stepped from the car and stood on the gravel watching the pair of diggers adding to their piles of dirt.

"Ivan's had the old swings torn up," Sally said.

"Well I can see that."

"He's turning it into housing."

"Really?" Julia gasped.

"Mmhmm." Sally nodded. "Four homes, apparently."

Julia couldn't help but think there was a hint of smugness in how Sally drip-fed the information to her.

One of Julia's hands moved to her hips, the cold wind blowing in off the moors temporarily forgotten as she stood there, gobsmacked. It seemed incredibly incongruous for houses to spring up here. The Barley Mow had always marked the edge of the village, with only a few small and isolated farms beyond it, the moors running unbroken for miles. It didn't seem right that there might be a street of homes, even one of just a few houses, with the streetlights and driveways and everything else that came along with them.

"Come on," Sally said, motioning towards the pub. "We'd better get going or we'll be late."

With a last glance towards the building work, Julia allowed herself to drift after Sally.

"I'm amazed he got planning permission," Julia said absentmindedly as she trailed alongside.

Sally let out a snort. "You'll have to ask Ivan about that," she said.

"What does that mean?"

Sally didn't reply, she kept walking while her face, Julia felt, went deliberately enigmatic. "Just ask him," she said.

Julia scowled, watching the curls on the back of her friend's head bounce as she strode ahead and went through the small wooden door of the Barley Mow.

Julia followed her inside, stepping into the snug parlour, which sat separate from the pub's dining room. The ceiling was low, the oak beams making it lower still, although Julia could still stand upright beneath them, just. Broad flagstones underfoot, worn smooth over the years, stretched away to the bar.

As Julia hung her coat on the peg by the door, the room felt almost icy cold and a gust of wind rattled the window panes at that moment as though to emphasize the point. However, she knew that once the customers started packing in and the fire got going, the pub was going to be swelteringly hot.

The door behind the bar at the far side of the room banged open and Ivan entered, holding a plastic tray stacked precariously with empty pint glasses, still dripping from the dishwasher. A long, striped apron protected the starched white shirt underneath that strained against his middle-aged bulk. Noticing his two staff, he set the tray down on the top of the bar with a rattle of glass. He looked out of breath and slightly red in the face, evidently he'd been bustling about as usual in preparation of opening the doors.

"Hi, girls," Ivan said, leaning heavily forward on the bar as he caught his breath. He looked like he was struggling for words, he ran a hand through his rapidly thinning hair and his mouth opened and closed a couple of times before he spoke again. "I was terribly sorry to hear about Barry. And that you had to be the one to find him, Julia."

Julia mumbled something along the lines of a thank you, just as unsure as Ivan was of how to go about this conversation.

Luckily, Ivan saved her by continuing on. "I feel rather bad now, for some of the things I said about him yesterday."

Julia guessed this was aimed more at Sally than at her, as she still wasn't sure exactly what Ivan had said about the late waiter yesterday. It didn't take a genius to realize it had been rather colourful, though.

"I was never all that fond of the lad, truth be told, but, well, you know."

Julia did know. Someone being workshy and tardy didn't mean that you wanted to see them dead. She hoped.

This time the conversation did stall, and the three of them stood in awkward silence, avoiding catching each other's eyes for what felt like an incredibly drawn-out moment. Eventually, the wind picked up again, this time, carrying with it the beeping sound of heavy machinery reversing.

"I gather you've started building work out there," Julia said, motioning past Ivan in the direction of the rear garden.

"Yes, yes, that's right," Ivan said, glancing over his shoulder as though he would somehow see the construction work through the two solid stone walls that intervened. He had a proud glow on his face when he turned back. "Soon to be four brand-new homes. And hopefully four more families to become regular patrons of the Barley Mow."

Julia had to hand it to the man, he had an uncanny scent for profit. Briefly, her mind drifted back to Mark, who would already be hard at work on the bookshop, trying to make sure it was all fit and ready to go before their opening. She had a twinge of guilt that she wasn't there helping, but still, every penny earned here would be another penny for the war chest they'd need if they were going to make a decent fist of the shop.

"Julia was just asking me about the planning permission," Sally said innocently. "But you know, I couldn't remember all the details. Too complicated for me!"

Julia scowled at Sally, who was obviously stirring the pot in one way or another, but whatever game she was playing was lost on Ivan whose face split into an ear-to-ear grin.

"That's the best thing about it!" he said, gleefully. "Because I'm only replacing the old coach house, I don't need any planning permission. With it being an existing structure and all."

Julia's mind whirred through the motions as she struggled to make sense of this. The old coach house rang a very distant bell in her memory. Dimly, she could recall a tumbledown, weed-choked stone building being there when she was a child, its roof long since fallen in. If she remembered correctly, it had been a favourite for the more daring children to go exploring in, although she herself had been a bit too young for that. She had only been about thirteen years old when the thing was bulldozed and the swing set put up in its place which, in one swoop, provided the children with a place to play and removed the liability payout that was waiting to happen. Of course, the children had all spurned the swings for other, more dangerous pastimes instead.

"But that coach house hasn't existed in at least a decade," Julia said, before she could help herself.

Ivan's grin disappeared briefly but soon came back, even if it seemed slightly forced. "On the official plans it's still there," he said, waving a meaty hand towards the back of the pub. "Hence: existing structure; hence: no planning permission needed. And as of yesterday, whatever may or may not have been there has been cleared away, so no one could ever know if it was a coach house or, say, an old set of swings. But, do you know, in all my years as landlord I can't recall ever seeing children playing on swings in the beer garden so it surely must have been a coach house that was there. Right?"

"Right," Julia murmured her agreement, not really knowing whether that argument would wash with the parish council but knowing perfectly well where her pay cheque came from.

Ivan clapped his hands together. "Anyway, I need to get on with work, and I'm sure you two do as well. Lots to do to get two lunch services organized," he said, and with that he disappeared back through the door he'd come from and into the staff corridor that ran behind the bar.

Julia gave Sally a questioning glance as they made their way after him. "I meant to ask you about that," she said.

Sally hummed. "Ivan's giving the workmen some discount on their lunch if they have it at three o'clock, after the main lunch service finishes."

Julia again felt a wave of admiration for the landlord. Paying the workers and then recouping a chunk of the wages in food and beer. He'd have been at home running a Victorian company store, that's for sure. As she grabbed her apron and started tying it on, she wondered if flogging local history books and true-crime novelizations at the bookshop would require her to be just as ruthless.

Julia's musings were cut short by a loud crash coming from the kitchens.

Ivan broke into a short run, his meaty hand flying out to push the kitchen door open and Julia and Sally followed him through.

The chef, Rob, stood in the middle of the cramped kitchen; a stack of shattered plates laid at his feet.

He was red in the face and shaking, his hands clutched at his breast. He was a blonde-haired man, a little shorter than Ivan in height, and in his late twenties – a few years older than Julia. He looked up as they arrived, obviously doing his best to hold back tears.

"I'm sorry," he whimpered, eyes flickering down to the plates he'd destroyed.

Ivan placed his hands on his hips, although the narrow galley kitchen barely afforded him the room to do so, and looked from Rob to the plates and back. "Get a grip, lad, it's only some plates. They'll come out of your wages easily enough."

"Ivan," Julia said softly, squeezing herself past him. "I think Rob's probably upset about something other than the broken plates."

She squeezed down the galley kitchen to Rob. "Were you very close to Barry?" she asked him.

Rob sniffed and turned away rather than face her. "No," he said. "But it's just so horrible, you know?" His hands fluttered up briefly, not knowing what to do with themselves before he knotted his fingers together to keep them still.

"Perhaps it's best if you took the day off?" Sally said.

"A day off? With double lunch service this afternoon?" Ivan spluttered.

Julia spun on her heel and glared at him. It wasn't often she stood up to her boss but it seemed to have the desired effect because the landlord deflated like a balloon.

"Yes, yes, of course," Ivan muttered. "You get yourself home. I'll ring around and see who's available."

Rob snatched his coat from the hook and made for the back door. He paused on his way out. "Thanks," he said, shooting a quick glance at Julia.

"It's all right," Ivan said. "Now go on, before I change my mind."

Rob took his advice and slipped out of the building, the door clicking softly behind him.

Sally sighed. "I'll fetch a broom," she said.

* * *

The final diner rose from their chair, burped, and waddled their way in the direction of the exit with a wide smile and wider belly.

Glancing down at her phone, Julia saw it was quarter to three. She nodded politely to the diners as they passed by and then crossed the dining room to collect the pair of coffee cups sitting on the food-stained tablecloth. As she picked them up, she saw a shining pair of pound coins which she swept into the pocket of her apron where HMRC would never find them.

Blowing out the candle, she wove her way between the tables and through the door into the parlour where she nudged Sally out of the way using her hip and pulled the dishwasher open, depositing the coffee cups inside.

"Is that the last of them?" Sally asked.

"Yep," Julia replied as she closed the dishwasher again, straightening up and stretching out her aching back. Sally had not been lying when she had said lunch was manic at the pub right now. How they'd coped yesterday a person down she didn't like to think.

Although, glancing up at the parlour now the lunch rush was done, the pub was completely empty. It often was these days.

Sally pushed open the door to the kitchens and called through. "We're going on our break now, Ivan, all right?"

"No." The reply came shouted back.

With wordless agreement, Julia and Sally ignored him, as they always did, and made their way through the narrow, crooked corridor towards the rear exit of the pub.

As they stepped out into the wintry air, the workmen from the construction site were filing past in the other direction. They were composed of a dozen or so men in mud-slicked hi-vis jackets, trooping by in twos or threes exchanging jokes or gossip as they went. Julia couldn't help but notice that one or two of them sent bashful smiles towards Sally as they passed. Of course they did.

As the door closed behind the last of them, Julia and Sally took up a perch on one of the trio of picnic benches that sat on the paving stones at the back of the Barley Mow. The dark wood was still slightly damp to sit on, it had evidently been raining while they'd been inside working, but now the sun was doing its best to make an appearance, bathing the pub's beer garden and the fields beyond it in a pale, yellow light.

Julia considered the view as she stretched her legs out and did her best to wiggle her toes inside her work shoes. The beer garden had really never been much. It was comprised of long, unkempt grass that was studded all over with little mounds of anthills and most of the year with dandelions, too. But uninspired as it was, the view wasn't improved at all by the addition of a pile of broken concrete and a mound of raw earth at the far end, nor by the two bright orange diggers perched at an alarming-looking angle beside it.

Come to think of it, Julia didn't think the view would be improved by four new houses, either, but that was Ivan's business, she supposed. Still, she couldn't help wondering about how the fine people who lived there were going to access their homes, or what would happen to whatever was flushed out of their toilets, given the planning people at the council apparently hadn't been consulted, or indeed informed. But, again, that was Ivan's business.

A thick cloud of strawberry-flavoured vapour curled in front of Julia's face and she wrinkled her nose, turning to see Sally puffing deeply on a vape pen.

"Since when do you vape?" Julia asked, nodding towards the device in her friend's hand.

Sally tilted her head up to blow another cloud into the air and then studied the pen as though seeing it for the first time. "It's an early birthday present," she said.

"From who?" Julia asked her.

"From you," Sally replied, her face a picture of innocence as she drew another deep breath.

"I don't really recall getting it for you," Julia said dryly.

"No," Sally agreed. "But I thought if I went and bought it, it would save you the trouble."

Julia cast her mind back to the various rather crummy Christmas and birthday presents she'd bought her friend when money had been tight, which was always, and decided that she couldn't really blame her for taking matters into her own hands.

They sat for a few moments in silence as the occasional raised voice drifted past from inside the pub and one or two cars made their way down the country lane, the sound of their engines carrying a long way across the quiet of the moorland.

"Do you remember when Ivan put those swings in?" Sally asked, glancing in the direction of the twisted metal poles that lay discarded next to the earthworks.

Julia shrugged. She had plenty of fond memories of coming here with her family as a child and playing in the garden with the other kids. But she seemed to remember they all avoided the swings for some reason.

"Mostly I just remember Ivan getting irate because none of the kids would go on them," Julia said.

"Yes, because they were haunted," Sally said, lowering her voice to sound serious.

Julia let out a laugh. "Yes, I'd forgotten they were meant to be haunted," she said.

"Not 'meant to be', they *were* haunted," Sally insisted. "They used to swing all by themselves, because the ghost was on them."

"And definitely not just blowing in the wind," Julia said. Sally ignored her, so she carried on. "I can't remember any of us actually playing on them, but we used to dare each other to run up and touch them, didn't we?"

"And then we'd all run away screaming because we thought the ghost was after us."

"That's right," Julia said. "And Barry was always the biggest scaredy cat of them all, bless him. He'd never touch them."

"He'd never go anywhere near them," Sally agreed.

They both lapsed into silence again at the mention of Barry's name. The wind blew and Sally puffed once again on her newly acquired vape pen.

"It was just as well we never played on them anyway," Julia said. "Ten-foot-high swings with solid concrete underneath them to fall onto. They were probably no safer than the crumbling old coach house they replaced."

Sally smiled. "They knew how to build play equipment in our day, didn't they?"

"They sure did. None of this rubber-crumb safety stuff that kids have today, was there?"

"Soft. That's what today's kids are," Sally said.

"They don't know the meaning of hard work."

"Speaking of, I think we were due back ten minutes ago."

"Oh, probably." Julia sighed and stood up from the bench, ignoring the wet feeling on her backside. At least her trousers were already dark so it wouldn't show. "Whose ghost was it anyway? That we used to think haunted the swings."

"Oh, that was—" Sally was interrupted, something over by the diggers catching her attention. "Hang on a minute, what's that?"

Chapter 4

At the far end of the beer garden, a figure came dashing out from between two cars in the car park and sprinted across the sodden grass in the direction of the building site.

It was impossible to discern their features, especially at this distance, because they had the hood of their pale grey jumper pulled up over their head.

They vaulted over the discarded poles of the old swing set, and began pounding up the side of the excavated earth, their legs working overtime to fight against the crumbling slope. Reaching the pinnacle, they began a semi-controlled descent down to the far side, at one point slipping to their knees as the earth shifted beneath them, but quickly regaining their balance and continuing on.

It apparently hadn't occurred to them that it would have been easier to go around.

Once on the far side they resumed their run, sprinting another half-dozen or so paces and then launching themselves up into one of the small diggers, clearing the caterpillar tracks in one go and grabbing hold of the roll bars of the cab in order to haul themselves in.

Sally watched the figure's progress, mouth agape. "Is that one of the construction guys?" she managed finally.

"I don't think so," Julia said, equally transfixed by the bizarre show they were watching. "No hi-vis and I didn't recognize the clothes. Besides, have you ever known a workman who looked that keen to get back from lunch?"

"Forgot their phone, maybe?" Sally ventured.

Watching the person flailing manically about inside the digger, it seemed rather unlikely. After a couple of seconds of frantic action, there came the sound of an engine and the vehicle shuddered into life.

"I'm pretty sure they're up to no good," Julia said, eyes still glued to the scene. "I think you should go and fetch the builders."

It took Sally a few more moments to tear herself away, but she let her vape pen drop to the picnic table and went beetling back inside.

As Julia watched, the digger pivoted one way and then back the other. The arm clawed at the empty air before eventually lowering into the trench and scooping the earth up, depositing the dirt it hauled up here and there on either side of it.

The door of the pub came flying open, and the dozen or so members of the construction crew came flowing out onto the patio with Sally and Ivan swept along in their midst.

"Just what is going on here?" one of the men demanded. He was a short, solidly built man with an impressively bushy black beard that framed his whole face. That face was rapidly turning bright red with fury as he watched the machine jerk this way and that, clods of earth flying as it did so.

"Is he one of yours?" Julia asked, motioning at the hooded driver in the cab.

The bearded man spluttered. "One of mine? One of mine?"

The chap next to him, a more slightly built man with fiery ginger stubble, answered a little more coherently on his friend's behalf. "We're all present and accounted for," he said, glancing quickly around at the assembled men to double-check.

The men themselves stood clustered on the patio, all talking over each other in rising voices as they watched the digger's labours in the trench. One or two seemed angry, but the majority were treating this as a form of free lunchtime entertainment and laughed and nudged one another in the ribs. One man nipped back inside and fetched his pint from the dining room, leaning back against the wall of the pub to enjoy the show.

The bearded man, who Julia realized was likely the foreman, rounded on them. "Well, don't just stand there!" he bellowed. "Go and stop them, for pity's sake."

"Why stop him? Looks like he's doing our work for us," the builder beamed and took another pull on his pint.

The foreman glared at him and the builder stopped beaming, although it took visible effort to do so.

There was a general exchange of looks as the workers tried to decide who cared enough, or was being paid enough, to go and intervene with whatever shenanigans were ongoing at the end of the beer garden, but the jovial laughter had died down.

Eventually the ginger-stubbled man slumped his shoulders in defeat as a couple of his companions gave him a firm push in the direction of the earthworks. "Go on, Charlie," one of them called, giving him a final shove to help him on his way.

The reluctant Charlie hopped up from the patio to the uneven lawn and began to run. Slowly at first, but gaining speed as he warmed to his task, encouraged by one or two calls from his friends behind him and, Julia noted, from Sally.

A couple of the other construction workers followed in Charlie's wake, being sure not to run so fast that they might overtake him before he reached the digger.

Just before he did so, the digger took one final, deep scoop of earth and then the whole construction vehicle turned on its tracks and began to jolt away towards the farmland beyond the beer garden.

Jeers came up from the audience and those in pursuit increased their pace but it was obviously futile. The digger was easily outpacing them, bumping and swaying as it crossed the beer garden, leaving deep brown gashes in the grass as it serpentined along.

It would seem, however, that the digger had made a tactical blunder. A dozen yards away along its path was the stout, shoulder-height wooden fence that separated the pub from the fields beyond.

Undaunted, the digger reached the barrier and crashed through. The bucket, still laden with the final scoop of soil, made contact first and the splintering of the wood was audible even from the patio. The bulk of the machine followed after, forcing the horizontals apart and continuing on into the field. A flock of crows rose from further down the fence, taking noisily to the air as their perch collapsed beneath them.

"Who's paying for that fence, then?" Ivan said darkly. Everyone roundly ignored him.

The digger bumped along for another thirty seconds and then came to an abrupt halt. Julia realized it had reached the drainage rhyne at the far end of the field. A murmur went round the audience as others came to the same conclusion.

Slowly the digger turned through ninety degrees, as the workmen chasing it closed the ground to roughly half the length of the field. The red-haired builder who was leading the charge got agonizingly close, almost within grasping distance before the digger was off again, striking out sideways. Its pursuers, now looking rather out of breath, straggled along behind.

The digger accelerated off, mud flying from its whirling tracks, putting green space between itself and the chasing workforce again. But within mere seconds it had reached the other ditch that bounded the side of the field and halted once more.

A ragged cheer swept up from the audience around Julia but it quickly died away.

"Oh my word, he's going for it," Julia heard Sally whisper, grudging admiration in her voice.

With a roar of its engine, a plume of black exhaust was belched into the air and the digger jerked forward again. It ploughed on into the rhyne and with a spray of water disappeared from sight, only the raised arm still peeking up above the ditch, empty bucket hanging limply. The arm wobbled and swayed side to side, but there was undeniable movement forward, too, and then the vehicle emerged again on the far side, leaning back at a precarious angle as it fought its way up the bank.

The cheer began to swell again in the audience but was cut short.

"Don't you dare cheer that," the foreman rasped. Obediently, his charges lapsed into silence.

As they looked on, the digger climbed almost all the way up the bank and then gravity caught up with it, stalling its progress. There was a collective groan as the digger came to a halt, then began tipping over backwards, its tracks spinning uselessly on the marshy slope. With a painful inevitability it toppled backwards in an ungainly arc, its arm embedding itself into the rhyne's bank on the near side as it came to rest upside down in the ditch with its tracks the only other part visible, still spinning. Julia heard a cry of anguish from the foreman beside her.

The digger's driver, whoever it was, appeared, abandoning the stolen vehicle and scrabbling on all fours up the side of the rhyne and out onto the far side, where they set off dripping across the field at an impressive pace.

Charlie reached the rhyne and came skidding to a halt, arms waving, like a show jumping horse refusing an obstacle. His colleagues came running up behind him, offering encouragement, and the man gave a valiant leap over the gap, clearing it but landing feet and hands in the sticky marsh on the far side. By the time he'd pulled himself free his quarry was just a distant shape, already disappearing into the hedging at the far side of the field. The builder threw his hands up in a show of resignation and turned back the way he had come.

"Right," the foreman announced. "Show's over. Hope you all enjoyed it. Back to work, everyone."

Julia could see his jaw clenched tight together as he fought to keep a lid on his anger.

"But I don't have a digger," one of his crew objected.

The foreman pointed at the remaining vehicle still at the construction site. "Get that one and go haul it out. Do I have to think of everything?"

With this the foreman stalked away across the beer garden, with his workforce following slightly after him.

The last workman peeled himself from his perch on the wall of the pub, his lager now almost empty. "But we never got our lunch," he called to the receding figure of the foreman. "Boss?"

"I'll get the girls to bring it out to you," Ivan said gruffly, and turned to go back inside.

* * *

It was only just past four o'clock, but already dark as night outside the windows. The workmen had downed tools a while back as the light had failed. Julia had peeked from the kitchen windows from time to time to watch them pull the stricken digger out of the rhyne by means of the other digger and a tow strap the foreman had produced from his van. The process had involved a lot of shouting, swearing and furious digging in the unrelenting mud of the bank and several of the workmen now wore mud-caked clothing as well as rather unhappy expressions on their faces.

Also unhappy was Ivan, who had stormed round the pub finding fault with almost everything he saw. Perhaps it was understandable he was in a foul mood; he'd lost a good chunk of work to simply recovering the digger from the ditch. The builders had barely resumed digging before the setting sun had put an end to it.

Still, around half the workforce had managed to find their way into the Barley Mow's parlour, drifting inside in dribs and drabs as they finished, and the tables by the log fire were now crowded with rapidly emptying beer glasses.

That, if nothing else, should buck Ivan's spirits a bit, Julia reflected.

She was perched on a stool by the bar clutching her handbag, keeping Sally company behind the bar while she waited for Mark to collect her. She looked up as the parlour door opened, but it was just a couple more of the builders trooping in, trailing clumps of mud behind them as they crossed to the bar.

Charlie, the red-haired man who had led the chase on the digger, arrived first, with a playful smile on his stubbled face. The cold and the mud apparently hadn't dampened his spirits. He looked between Sally and Julia, as though debating something. Eventually he pulled something from his pocket, and placed it on the top of the bar in front of Julia.

"Here," the man said. "Buried treasure for you."

Julia plucked the item from the bar and held it up at eye level. It was a delicate chain, at the end of which dangled a slender silver heart. It certainly didn't look new but it had a certain vintage-style charm to it, all the same. She brushed some specks of dirt away with her thumb and scrunched her face up, confused.

"Amazing what you find when you dig, isn't it?" Charlie's companion said before turning to Sally. "Two pints of best, please."

"Where's mine?" Sally asked, tilting her head at the necklace in Julia's hands.

"Just the one, sorry," Charlie replied. "Still, you could have my heart if you want."

Sally made a show of recoiling. "Nah, I'm good." She grabbed a glass from under the bar and hauled down on the pump, filling it more with foam than beer.

Julia was just examining the unusual gift, trying to decide if it was actually worth anything or not, when she realized someone had appeared at her shoulder.

Mark stood there, he'd snuck in quietly. His clothes were covered head to foot in streaks of paint. This was usually when he was at his happiest, but he didn't look to be in a particularly pleasant mood.

"What's that?" he asked, leaning in to look at the trinket in Julia's hand.

"Buried treasure," she replied automatically without thinking.

"Huh?"

"Never mind," Julia said. She looked down at the necklace in her palm one last time, its chain coiled around the heart. Then as casually as she could manage she tossed it towards Sally, who deftly plucked it from the air with one hand.

Without missing a beat, Sally looped the chain over her neck, the heart shining prominently against the stark black material of her work shirt. She flashed a smile across the bar at Charlie, who returned it. There were a couple of chuckles from his companions near the fireplace.

"Shall we go?" Julia said to Mark, sliding from the bar stool onto her aching feet. "I guess there's plenty to do at the shop."

Mark's brow was still furrowed as he stood trying to piece together what he'd just been witness to. "There always is," he sighed and turned to leave.

Mark put an arm around Julia as they left the pub. It made getting through the tiny wooden door awkward, but the affection was appreciated, at least.

"How was everyone?" Mark asked as they crossed the gravel of the car park towards his van. "With Barry, I mean."

Julia screwed her face up. "I think Ivan was probably more concerned with finding his replacement," she said.

Mark tutted in response.

"Rob was really cut up about it, though," she said.

"Rob?" Mark asked, untwining himself from Julia in order to pull the keys from his pocket.

"Yeah, you know Rob," Julia said. "One of the chefs. About your age. Quiet chap. Supports Arsenal but otherwise quite nice."

"Still not ringing any bells," said Mark.

"You met him at that lock-in a few weeks back. You talked to him about vans for a long time."

Mark shook his head. "I don't remember him," he said.

Julia scowled at him. "Probably don't remember much about that night the way you were putting them away."

Chapter 5

Mark cruised along Biddle's high street, somehow still clogged with traffic despite being late afternoon, before pulling the van up onto the pavement.

Julia hopped down just in time to catch a death stare from a young mum with a pushchair who had to traverse out onto the road to get around the newly arrived van, but she'd got mostly used to that sort of look since work had started renovating the shop.

The building itself had, until quite recently, been Biddle Rhyne's public library, as well as Julia's place of employment and her home away from home. They had been better days in many ways: plenty of quiet times to read, a small but reliable stream of income. But that was before the council had made the decision to defund the library and shut it down. After a few months of the building lying vacant and boarded up, and after some persuasion from Mark, too, they had put forward a proposal to turn it into a bookshop.

Given the circumstances, the rent had been a relative steal. The council, keen to be rid of what they considered an eyesore of a boarded-up property in the middle of their high street, had given them a discounted rate on condition they had the place fixed up and trading within two months.

All the same, Julia had still relied heavily on Mark's investment in order to cover the two months upfront the council had asked for, and one of those months had now almost entirely disappeared into converting the place into a shop.

Banners in the windows advertised that the shop would be 'opening soon'. Julia certainly hoped so.

She rustled around inside her handbag searching for the shop keys. Before she could find them, Mark edged past her and hurried in long strides up the short flight of stone steps to the door. He pulled his own keys from his pocket and opened it up. Julia rolled her eyes but followed him in, hoping her keys were actually in her handbag somewhere as she certainly didn't have any firm evidence that was the case.

She stepped through from the entry foyer and into the shop. The space looked larger now than it had as a library. That was the lack of shelves, Julia supposed. The room opened out on both sides of the door but the only fixture now was the counter, just to one side of it. For the time being, there was only empty space between that and the window at the far end. Well, not empty space, it was currently littered with a wide-ranging assortment of paint brushes and hand tools.

Mark hadn't been idle. What had been bare plaster only this morning was now a rich crimson. The colour of the paint had been chosen to match her living room. She had hoped the choice would have a calming effect.

Of course, the living room at home wasn't filled with acrid paint fumes. She did her best to filter that out, but it was really quite overwhelming and she felt her eyes start to water.

Mark read her face and looked crestfallen. "I thought you'd like it," he said. "I spent ages getting that shade of red right."

Julia laid a hand gently on his shoulder. "No, it's great, Mark, it is," she said, gazing around.

She couldn't fault the painting, but the room looked so tremendously bare. There were still no shelves, the counter was unfinished and the dust sheets crunching underfoot made the place look somehow derelict. It was hard to see this transforming into a functioning, not to say welcoming, shop in the space of just a few more weeks.

"Do you think it will all get done in time?" Julia asked.

"Oh, yes, definitely," Mark said, brimming with confidence.

"Really?"

"Yep. We might have to cut a few corners, but we'll get there," Mark said, casting an expert eye over the work in progress.

"What kind of corners?" Julia asked.

"Well, I probably won't bother painting the doors," Mark began, "and I'll leave the counter as unfinished rough wood. There might be a few splinters, but it will save us a good hour of work. And I don't think we'll have time to put shelves in so I thought you could just sort of stack the books up in heaps on the floor. In fact, it might be better if you don't sell books at all. I was thinking maybe turnips instead."

"Stop being silly," she said, and she couldn't help but feel a smile creeping on.

"Oh, but they love turnips around here, they'll fly off the shelves. Or off the heaps," Mark said, thickening his West-Country accent. "And I thought we could leave the ceiling unfinished. Like in those trendy bars."

"Now I know you're being silly," Julia said. "You've never been to a trendy bar."

Mark looked wounded. "No, but I've seen one on TV," he said. "It looked well good."

"Better than the Barley Mow?" Julia said.

"Way better. It was clean and shiny and it served all sorts of interesting drinks."

"But was there talent behind the bar?" Julia asked.

"Well, you've got me there," Mark admitted. "You can't beat the Barley Mow for bar staff."

They looked at each other, their eyes meeting. Mark smiled. "That Ivan is dreamy," he said.

Julia broke into laughter. Mark leaned in towards her but she pushed him gently away. "We've got work to do," she said. "The ceiling, for instance."

"Well, that can wait, but the walls should be dry enough for a second coat," he replied.

Julia sighed. She'd thought at least the walls were done, she hadn't realized there was another coat to come.

After the shift at the Barley Mow she would much rather be underneath a blanket with a book or Rumpkin or perhaps both. Or Mark, if he was particularly lucky.

But she knew there was work to be done, and every day they weren't trading was a day they were losing money, so she wriggled into her painting overalls and picked up a roller.

"If we get this done tonight, I should be able to get to fixing the shelves to the walls tomorrow," Mark said, grabbing his own roller and wetting it.

Julia nodded and set to work on the far wall. As she went, she tried to picture the place with shelves in. Once more her mind's eye saw the place packed with books and bustling with customers, perusing, enjoying and, most importantly, buying.

"Missed a bit." Mark's words snapped her out of her daydream.

Julia slapped some paint onto the errant patch of wall.

"So are you doing any more shifts at the pub?" Mark asked, without looking up from the paintwork.

His tone was easy but Julia knew there was a right and a wrong answer to the question and she trod carefully. "Well, Ivan wants me about as much as he can get me," she said.

"Does that mean you're working all week then?" Mark asked, just a little too curtly.

"I don't have to," Julia said, non-committal. "I'm sure they can cope without me, if you need me here."

"No, I don't need you," Mark said, still refusing to look round, working his roller manically up and down the wall. "In fact, once we're nearly done, I'll be keeping you away so you get the full effect of the final reveal."

Julia gave a little pause before she replied. "Then I guess I'll tell him I can do a few extra shifts and see what I squeeze in here around them."

Mark didn't reply, and reached for the paint-covered radio that was sitting on the dust sheets at his feet.

* * *

There was a rap at the door. Julia looked at Mark across the paint cans but she could tell from his face that he was just as bemused as she was. They placed their rollers back down and made their way to the little entrance hall just as the knocking came again.

Mark stepped forward, opened the door a crack and looked out onto the dark street.

"Oh, it's you," he said, the tension releasing from his broad shoulders, and he opened the door fully and stood aside.

His dad walked in, his hair all askew on top of his head from the wind outside. He glanced through the doorway at the ongoing work in the next room.

"I thought I might find you here, Julia," he commented. "I had a couple more questions to ask you about Barry."

Julia wiped her hands on her overalls, smearing red across her torso. "What did you want to know?" she asked.

"Well," the inspector said, ambling a few wide steps into the next room, looking around him as he did so. "It was here at the library that you saw Barry, is that right? And he was on his way to catch the bus back from work?"

"Yes," Julia replied.

Jones nodded thoughtfully. "We've had a chance to talk to all Barry's neighbours now, and it seems you were probably the last person to see him alive. I'll need to know your movements for the rest of that day, Julia."

"It's Mark!" Julia blurted out suddenly.

"Huh?" Jones turned to face her properly for the first time since he entered, confusion written all over his face.

"My… alibi, I mean," Julia said, talking breathlessly. "I was with Mark. First here in the shop, then he spent the night at mine and then after working on the shop again we went to the garden centre together to get supplies, and then we went straight from there to Barry's house. I was with Mark the whole time. You can ask him."

Jones scoffed. "I'm just trying to put a timeline together. I wasn't accusing you of murder."

"Again," Mark added, quietly.

"What was that, Son?"

"You weren't accusing her of murder *again*." There had been a rather unfortunate misunderstanding between Julia and the Detective Inspector after Audrey White had been killed.

Jones at least had the good grace to look sheepish. "Right. Well, I'm not accusing anyone of anything at the moment. I'm just trying to get the facts straight. Do you remember what time Barry passed by here?"

"About ten in the evening?" Mark ventured, looking to Julia for confirmation.

She nodded.

"Mhhm, okay," the inspector said.

Julia noticed his hand twitching for his notebook but it seemed he was trying to keep the interview informal and taking mental notes instead.

Jones reached into his jacket pocket and pulled out a sheet of paper which he unfolded and placed onto the unsecured wood of the shop's counter. He smoothed the sheet down. It looked like a still from CCTV taken inside a bus.

"Do you recognize anyone in this picture?" Jones asked.

Julia's finger darted out, landing triumphantly on the paper. "That's Barry!"

Jones's eyes narrowed slightly. "Yes, I know that's Barry," he said. "I mean, do you recognize anyone else?"

"Oh," said Julia, realizing that the inspector must have pulled this still of Barry on his way home. She looked down at the photo again. The bus was only sparsely occupied, a few people scattered here and there on the seats, none of them particularly close to Barry. She didn't recognize any of them, although it wasn't the clearest image. "No," she said, "but what's that?"

She pointed on the picture to the rear window. It was pixelated and hard to make out, but it looked like a small white car was on the road behind the bus.

"Our mystery car?" said Jones.

Mark squinted at the picture. "Looks like it could be," he said.

Jones picked the paper up again and examined it closely before folding it back away. "Still no number plates," he said.

Now his notebook did come out and he scrawled something down. "I'll talk to the driver and see if he remembers anything. Now, you said last night at the scene that you couldn't think of anyone who would have done it. Are you sure you can't think of anyone that might have wanted to harm Barry?"

"No." Julia shook her head, although her conscience was tugging at her.

"All right, then. Thanks for your time, I'll let you get back to the painting." Jones gave a final look at the half-finished walls and began heading for the front door.

"Actually, there is someone," Julia said, stopping Jones in his tracks. "Or rather, two someones."

Jones turned and looked at her, his eyes piercing, but she hesitated. "Yes?" he prompted.

Julia sighed and slumped her shoulders. She really didn't want to go down this route, and her gut instinct told her there was no way they would have been capable of hurting Barry. But then again, her gut instinct had led her astray before.

DI Jones cleared his throat meaningfully.

"Lance and Janice Teller," Julia murmured softly.

An eyebrow arched on the inspector's face. The notepad reappeared, deftly flicked from his jacket pocket, pen already in the other hand. "Really? And why might they have reason to cause Barry harm?"

Julia squirmed but it was no good, she'd started this now. "Barry had an affair with Janice," she said, unable to meet the inspector's eyes. "A few months ago, now."

"And was Lance aware of this? To the best of your knowledge?" Jones asked.

"Janice told me that she was going to tell him everything. As far as I know she did."

Jones nodded thoughtfully as he scribbled on his pad. "Well, I guess I'll need to pay the Tellers a little visit," he said. He seemed buoyed that he now had a suspect, someone to pin it on.

Julia remembered all too well the feeling of being in the inspector's sights.

He made to go again but Julia called after him. "Inspector…"

"Yes?" Jones asked, half turning to look over his shoulder at her.

"Please tread carefully with Janice. She's a lovely woman really, and very delicate. I'm sure she wouldn't hurt anyone. And Lance has such a temper."

The policeman's eyes gleamed at this last statement and instantly Julia wished she could take the words back. It was true she'd seen him blustering and raging before, and Julia could tell that Janice was at least slightly afraid of her husband, but as far as she knew, he'd never been violent towards anyone.

"Maybe I could talk to her first? Get a feel for things without upsetting anyone too much?" Julia suggested.

"Let you go off and interview a suspect, a suspect in a murder enquiry, possibly tipping them off before I arrive?" Jones shook his head slowly. "I'm fond of you, Julia, I really am, and I know this is a rather emotional time for the whole village. But I'm warning you, and I'll say this only once, don't poke around in this. I don't want any interference."

Julia bit her lip but didn't reply, and so with that the inspector took his leave.

As the door closed behind him, Mark laid a gentle hand on Julia's shoulder. "You did the right thing in telling him," he said.

"I hope so," Julia replied, listening to the sound of Jones's car roaring away down the high street.

She should heed Jones's advice, she knew. She had no business prying into a murder investigation. On the other hand, if she hadn't intervened before, there was every likelihood that Mrs White's killer would still be at large and she herself might well be behind bars.

* * *

It was late by the time Julia finally made it home, aching from top to toe.

No dog bounded out to greet her as she kicked her shoes off. It would seem that the gas fire was still winning the battle for Rumpkin's affections. She made a mental note to give him a good, long walk as soon as time allowed. A sort of counteroffensive.

She'd barely eaten all day and on the way home had thoughts of making a sandwich, but judging by the smell drifting out of the kitchen Sally had been baking which seemed like a far, far better prospect.

"Sally?" Julia bellowed.

"Kitchen!" The reply came back.

Three things struck Julia as she pushed through the kitchen door.

First, the heat of the oven that hit her like a wave.

Second, the smell of cinnamon, which was so thick she fancied that she could see clouds of the stuff floating in the air.

Third, the stranger leaning against the kitchen counter at the far end of the room.

"Oh, hello." Julia stopped in her tracks.

Sally's front half retracted itself from the open oven and straightened up, clutching a tray of perfectly golden muffins. "This is Charlie," she said. "From the construction crew, remember?"

Julia blinked. Now Sally mentioned it, she recognized the wiry, ginger-haired man.

"We just got talking after he'd finished work. It turns out we were at the same school, he was a few years above," Sally said. She whipped her baking apron off revealing the fitted grey T-shirt underneath. Evidently today she'd found time to change after coming back. Still hanging against her chest was the heart-shaped pendant that Charlie had given her, in a roundabout way.

Sally brushed a stray curl of hair free from her face and Julia noticed endearing patches of flour that had settled on her cheek. She'd almost certainly placed them there deliberately for effect.

Charlie stuck out a hand and Julia shook it. "So, you're helping get rid of the swings then," she said.

"That's right," Charlie nodded. "Not that we made much progress today, with everything that went on."

"Yeah, I saw you chasing that digger," Julia said, recalling the image of the man charging valiantly across the field. "What was that about?"

Charlie gave a shrug. There was a twinkle in his eyes as though he'd enjoyed the whole affair. "Just a bored kid, I guess. It's probably best that we didn't catch him, Ed would have given him an absolute hiding."

"Did it set you back much?" Julia asked.

"Nah," Charlie said. "Just today really, the digger's no worse for wear now we've got it out and the right way up again. We still ought to finish next week, weather permitting."

"Finish?" Julia said.

"We're just clearing the ground," Charlie explained. "Someone else will be building the actual homes."

"Ah, I see."

"I can remember those swings going up," continued Charlie. "It's funny tearing them down. Makes me feel old. I used to play on them as a lad."

"Did you actually play on them?" Julia asked. "We were always too scared."

"Right," said Charlie. "On account of the ghost."

"Right."

Sally finished placing the last of the muffins onto a cooling wire. "Charlie was one of the brave ones," she said, a hint of pride in her voice.

"It's true," Charlie said, puffing his chest out. "I wasn't afraid of no ghosts."

Julia smiled at him then turned to Sally. "Whose ghost was it meant to be, anyway? Do you remember?"

Sally stroked her chin, dislodging a small amount of flour in the process. "Wasn't it Aimiee West's?"

"That's right," Charlie said. "I remember her well; she was in my year."

"Oh, yeah." That name took Julia back. "I'd forgotten all about that. She went missing just around the time the swings were put up, didn't she?"

"Exactly," Sally said.

"So, obviously, she would haunt the swings that she never went on," Charlie said.

Julia opened her mouth to chuckle but a long yawn came out instead. "Excuse me," she said. "I'm absolutely beat. I think I'll take one of those and I'll retire up to my room."

She took a step forward and reached in past Charlie to pull one of the warm muffins from the cooling rack. She couldn't help noticing Charlie stare at her as she did so.

"Sorry, don't mean to be rude, are you bleeding?" Charlie said, gesturing at the side of Julia's face.

She reached up and touched her skin, feeling the paint flaking underneath her fingers and laughed. "It's just paint," she said and explained about the bookshop conversion.

From behind Charlie, Sally gave a meaningful cough.

"Right," Charlie said. "Sounds like a lot of work. Well, perhaps if we get any days rained off I could stick my head in and lend a hand, or something."

Julia suppressed a smile. Behind the stilted speech she could sense Sally tugging at the strings. "That would be very kind," she said. "Anyway, I really should get up to bed. Nice to meet you, goodnight."

Julia could hear the muffled sounds of conversation as she closed the kitchen door behind her and made her way upstairs.

Once she reached her room, she put the radio on and started getting changed ready for bed. She was stiff all over and it was a welcome relief to get into her pyjamas. Normally the room was freezing cold at this time of year, but the heat from the kitchen had risen up and warmed it through nicely, so she lay on top of the duvet until the local news came on.

Unsurprisingly, Barry's murder was the leading story, taking precedence over arguments about the bus routes into King's Barrow and whether the schools were performing as expected – they were not.

The report concluded by interviewing Jones about the case. In his usual laconic style, the inspector gave very little away about what had happened, but he did ask for anyone with information about seeing a white Micra in the area at the time to contact the police.

Julia flicked the radio off, crawled beneath the blankets and sighed as she shut her eyes. If only she and Mark had bothered to take note of the number plate, they might already know who the killer was.

Despite what Jones and Mark had said, she was going to keep her eyes out for that car.

Chapter 6

Julia drove into the Barley Mow's car park, past the pub sign which was still dripping wet from the morning's rain, and pulled up at the far end.

Dawn was just breaking, painting the underside of the dark cloudbanks a deep crimson and sending long shadows from the fenceposts stretching out over the nearby fields.

Taking a lungful of the morning air, she got out and opened the boot. Rumpkin bounced out and went sniffing around, tail wagging, while Julia struggled into her wellies and locked the car. By this time, Rumpkin had already got bored and squirmed underneath the fence, caking his underside in mud as he went. Julia could see him disappearing off across the field.

With a sigh, she went after him. Rather than go back out to the lane and walk to the gate, she hopped the fence where she was, straddling it awkwardly before managing to land with a squelch on the other side, and headed over the grass towards the footpath. With each step, her boots sank ankle-deep into the ground and she muttered some choice phrases about her pet as she did her best to stride after him.

Still, she had been promising him a decent walk to make up for all the time kept cooped up at home while she was out working or painting, which seemed to be always at the moment, and this walk was one of his favourites. Watching the animal zip happily back and forth through the long grass at least somewhat made up for hauling herself out of bed before sunrise and driving down.

She ploughed on through the mud until she reached the footpath that ran parallel to the rhyne, although after a long winter even the path had been churned into deep mud. Her short walk had brought her level with the Barley Mow's beer garden. The diggers sat alongside the mounds of dirt, their scoops hanging motionless in the air. Apparently both the builders and their machines got a lie-in on a Saturday, unlike dog owners. Julia couldn't decide if she wanted the homes to go ahead for Ivan's sake or get slapped down for the sake of, well, she wasn't quite sure. Preserving the village, she supposed, which had surely reached absolute perfection when her and Sally's own house was built in the 1970s. Or was it the 1980s?

She pulled her wellie free from a particularly bad patch of mud on the path and realized that she couldn't see Rumpkin anymore. She stood with her hands on her hips and looked around for him.

"Where have you got to, you great lummox?" Julia's voice rang out over the moor and she turned around on the spot, scanning the long grass for any sign of the creature.

Nerves began to set in, an itchy feeling on the nape of Julia's neck. Rumpkin was a great one for disappearing to investigate things but it was unlike him not to come back when she called.

Suddenly the grass between her and the rhyne rustled violently and Rumpkin's head popped over the top, springing up to see where she was and then charging along through it until he arrived at her feet.

"There you are," Julia said, bending down to pat him.

The dog looked up at her with loving eyes. There was something in his mouth.

"What's that you've got there?" Julia said. "Drop."

Rumpkin hesitated, unwilling to give up whatever he was holding. But after a moment of deliberation he scrunched down on his haunches and opened his mouth, depositing it onto the ground by his mistress's feet.

Julia nudged it with the toe of her boot. It was a bone.

She stood staring at it, a queasy feeling rising in her stomach. On its own, the fact it was a bone wasn't too bad. It could just mean that a sheep had died around here. But Julia parked by these fields every few days or so. She couldn't recall the last time there had been sheep in them. Last spring, maybe.

"Where did you find this?" she asked Rumpkin.

With infuriating predictability, the animal just sat looking up at her perplexed and cocked his head to one side.

Julia swallowed. She hoped she was wrong, but she thought she could guess where the bones had come from.

Clipping Rumpkin's lead on, Julia broke off from the footpath and pushed through the grass, heading straight across the field to the rhyne. At first Rumpkin protested, not wanting to be separated from his find. But when he realized where Julia was going, he bounded on ahead, pulling sharply on the lead as he strained to go faster.

When they reached the bank, Rumpkin barked excitedly and tried to scamper down the edge until Julia tugged him back and peered in for herself. There was a large clump of earth piled in there, effectively splitting the low, still water into two. Poking out in a couple of places were little white protrusions of bone. They could easily have passed for animal bones. But lying just next to them, beneath the surface of the shallow water was a skull. A human skull.

Julia tore her eyes from it and looked at the muddy bank. There was a thick track gouged into the ground, disappearing from view as it entered the long grass. The tracks of a digger. It was only too obvious what had happened. The runaway digger that had been stolen the previous day had fled this way across the field, then dumped the earth into the rhyne, bones and all.

The body, whoever it was, had come from the Barley Mow.

Still fighting to bring Rumpkin under control, Julia plunged her free hand into her bag and felt around until she found her mobile. She swore at herself. The battery was dead, she'd forgotten to charge it last night.

"Come on, boy," she commanded, giving a final tug on the lead that brooked no argument and dragged the dog with her as she hurried through the slick grass towards the Barley Mow, making use of the hole in the fence the digger had created the day before.

She passed the quiet earthworks, not daring to spare a glance at the pit the bones must have come from, and let herself in through the kitchen door, the only one likely to be unlocked at this hour of the morning.

As she pushed through the door, the warmth of the kitchen hit her instantly. Ivan stood in the narrow room looking over the day's menu. His jaw pivoted open as he took in Julia's mud-covered boots and the equally filthy animal at her side.

"What on earth do you think you're doing?" he shouted, the colour already rising on his face. "Are you trying to make me fail my next health and safety inspection? Is this your idea of fun?"

Julia had been on the receiving end of enough of these outbursts that she could allow it to just wash over her.

"Ivan, I need to phone the police," she said, and pointed back out the way she'd come in. "There are bones out there in the field."

"Bones?" Ivan said.

"Human bones," Julia said.

"Good grief," Ivan said, eyes widening. "Go and use the phone behind the bar."

Muttering some quiet words of thanks, Julia dragged Rumpkin away from whatever he'd found to sniff in the corner of the kitchen and pulled him into the parlour, where she picked up the phone. She wasn't sure if 999 was the route to go for this, given the body was so old, so she got directory enquiries to put her through to the police station who then forwarded her onto Jones's mobile.

* * *

When she heard the sound of tyres on the gravel outside, Julia sprang from the barstool and hurried out through the parlour door, leaving Rumpkin tied to the brass footrest and protesting at his lot.

She emerged outside in time to see Jones manoeuvring himself out from his unmarked car and smoothing down his suit.

"Inspector," Julia called as she crossed the last couple of feet to meet him. "Thanks for coming so fast."

"I was in the area," Jones said, locking his car behind him. "Forensics shouldn't be too far behind. Show me what you've got then, Julia."

Julia led the way around the side of the building and traced her route back through the hole in the beer garden fence, following the digger's path towards the rhyne.

She couldn't quite bring herself to look at the bones again so she stood just back from the edge and pointed. "Down there."

Jones, seemingly unfazed that his smart trousers had been thoroughly ruined in their short walk over, trudged up the lip of the bank and looked down.

He turned back to Julia with his brow furrowed. "There's nothing there," he said.

"What?" Forgetting her earlier trepidation, Julia hurried up to join him on the bank and looked down.

Jones was right. There was the big clod of earth that the digger had deposited, but it was pointedly lacking in any bones.

"They were right there," Julia said, staring down at the silty water. "There was a whole skeleton and a human skull. You have to believe me."

Jones fixed Julia a look in the eye. "I do believe you," he said. "Unfortunately that means someone's been out here while you were waiting for me."

"But that was hardly ten minutes," Julia said.

Jones just gave a heavy shrug. "Who have you seen in the area today?"

"Only Ivan," Julia said. "But I'm certain he didn't leave the pub after I called you. The builders aren't in today."

Jones hummed thoughtfully to himself.

"Wait a moment," Julia said, as a thought hit her.

With a quick scan of the field to get her bearings, she jogged off into the grass, aware of the inspector following behind her like a badly hitched trailer.

She kept her eyes fixed on the ground as she went.

"There!" she said, triumphantly, pointing at the field ahead of her.

Jones carefully brushed past her and looked at where she was pointing.

The bone Rumpkin had retrieved still lay there, looking very small and unassuming in the grass. Jones gave a grunt. "Well, that's something," he said.

"Is it human?" Julia asked.

"I don't know. We have people for that," Jones said. As he spoke there was the sound of engines, a pair of marked Land Rovers drove down the road at the end of the field, heading towards the pub. "And it looks like they've arrived."

Jones peered down again at the single bone. "One more thing, Julia," he said.

"Yes?"

"Keep quiet about us finding this one," he said. "Whoever took the rest of the bones obviously didn't want us to find it. It might be best that they think they've got their wish."

Julia nodded. "Okay."

* * *

The forensic team were hard at their work in the rhyne with thick, black rubber boots pulled on over their white suits, face masks and hoods anonymizing all of them. They made a methodical advance through the water looking for any more bones, but so far they hadn't turned anything up.

They had quite an audience. DI Jones stood on the bank, shoes sinking into the mud and hands shoved into the pockets of his suit jacket. A dozen or so yards further along, Julia stood hugging herself for warmth. Further off, in the Barley Mow's beer garden, a crowd had gathered. A dead body was good for trade, it would seem. Punters clutched drinks and stood on top of the picnic benches trying to get a view of the activity, occasionally lifting a phone up in the air to photograph the goings-on.

Earlier, one of the forensic techs had done their best to bag the remaining bone and spirit it away, although just how surreptitious they could be in their billowing white outfit, Julia wasn't sure. Now they were making their way back across the field from the Land Rovers and after stamping the mud from their shoes they exchanged a few words with Jones before heading off again.

Jones turned and walked slowly along the side of the rhyne to Julia.

"We can't be certain yet, of course," Jones said by way of opening the conversation, "but the bone we do have would appear to be the thigh bone of a teenage girl. They've been buried for approximately ten years."

"It is Aimiee, then," Julia said. "She was under the swings that whole time."

Julia shivered and hugged herself closer still. That was an unsettling thought. At least they hadn't ever really played on them. The thought of having joyful childhood memories when there was a skeleton lurking underneath would have been too much.

"Were the two of you friends?" Jones asked.

"No, not really," Julia replied. "She was a bit older than me. We did play together a little, it's a small village, but I wouldn't have said we were friends."

Aimiee had only been sixteen when she went missing. That age difference had seemed huge back then, but it was only three years.

Jones nodded as Julia spoke, and she could tell he was taking mental notes for writing up later on.

"You worked the case, didn't you? When she went missing?" The inspector rarely talked about his work to Julia but she vaguely recalled Mark had mentioned it.

"I did," the inspector said. "We didn't have much to go on, though. She just didn't come home one evening, no trace of her. It wasn't clear if there was foul play or if she'd just decided to run off. No suspects in any case, although there was talk of a boyfriend. We looked for him at the time, but Aimiee had never told her parents his name, and it wasn't even clear if he was real or someone she'd made up. I don't suppose you remember anyone?"

"Sorry, Rhys, I don't," Julia said. She sniffed and found herself holding back tears and remonstrated with herself. It wasn't like she really knew the girl. "There were always stories, though, among the kids, that she was haunting the swing set. Someone must have known that she was buried there."

"Well, someone definitely knew she was buried there," Jones said. "Because they made an effort to dig her up before the workmen found her."

"Right, of course." Julia felt herself blushing. "I wasn't thinking straight, sorry."

"Don't be harsh on yourself, you've had an awful lot to process," Jones said.

Julia looked at the grass underfoot and didn't reply.

"I don't think we need anything more from you here," Jones said. He took a small step closer to her and spoke in a conspiratorial whisper, although there was no one even close to eavesdropping distance. "I'm not officially allowed to recommend this, of course. But if I were you, I'd go and have a nice, strong drink. It works wonders for me."

Julia sniffed again but managed a smile. "Thanks, Rhys," she said. "Maybe I will."

The inspector smiled back but then he looked over Julia's shoulder and it quickly melted away. "Oh, no," he muttered.

Julia glanced round to follow his gaze. "What is it?" she asked.

There was a man there, some way off, standing at the farm gate at the edge of the field as though unsure whether to cross it, his car parked in the entryway behind him.

"Who is it?" Julia asked, she watched the inspector closely but his expression gave little away.

He let a long breath out through his nose. "It's Graham West," he said quietly. "Aimiee's father."

"Oh," Julia said, looking up again.

He'd climbed the gate and was lowering himself down into the mud on the nearside.

"I had hoped we'd have a bit longer before he showed up," Jones said.

Julia looked over to the pub beer garden where people in the huddle were still doing their best to film the goings-on. "I guess word spreads fast." She wasn't sure where Aimiee's family had moved to, only that they'd left the area after it became clear that she wasn't going to come back.

"Well, I'd better go and tell him what's happened," Jones muttered as he started off through the grass to head the man off.

"Mr West," Jones called out as he neared him, the words just audible to Julia.

She didn't particularly want to stay to watch, but the two men were now between her and the way back to the road. She needed to collect Rumpkin from the parlour, but she'd rather not wade through the crowd of onlookers in the beer garden, so for now she waited.

Now he was closer, Graham West revealed himself to be a stout man with a circle of grey hair around his head. He was plainly dressed in khaki trousers and a button-down shirt. Judging from his smart shoes, now smeared with muck, he hadn't been expecting to tramp through a field when he set out that day.

Jones did his best to plant himself in the man's way, blocking his approach to where the forensic team were performing their work. One or two of the white-hooded technicians glanced up when they heard Jones's voice.

Mr West craned round to try and see over DI Jones's bulk. His face was a picture of frantic anguish. Julia supposed that even after all these years the pain could still be quite raw, especially with events like today's.

Jones had successfully managed to turn Mr West and he was ushering him back the way he had come from. A brief snatch of his words were carried to Julia on the wind. "We don't know anything for sure yet. Of course I'll let you know as soon as there's anything definite."

When Mr West got to his car, helped back over the five-bar gate by the inspector, he seemed to break down entirely, doubling over and raising his clenched fists to his face.

Jones put an arm around the man, and Julia couldn't help noticing that he put his body between Mr West and the crowd in the beer garden, shielding him from the cameras. Jones guided Mr West into the passenger seat of his own car.

Julia sighed and slowly made her way back along the side of the field towards the road. As she clambered over the gate to the roadside, Jones's car pulled away and she caught a glimpse of Mr West. He looked thoroughly wretched. She wondered if the detective had advised him to have a stiff drink, too.

* * *

Mark's van smelt delicious.

Safely nestled on the middle of the three seats up front was the piping hot bag of takeaway food.

But despite her stomach rumbling, Julia was hoping the journey would be endless.

She didn't enjoy the weekly visits to Mark's parents at the best of times. They had just about got over the initial awkwardness of the fact that his dad had arrested her on suspicion of Mrs White's murder, but she still wasn't exactly at ease around either parent.

And today would be so much worse, of course. Jones would have spent the day involved in the discovery of Aimiee West's bones, not a pleasant task by any stretch and unlikely to put him in a good mood. Julia wasn't feeling too perky either, after her morbid discovery of them.

Mark's initial attempts to cajole her into conversation had failed and most of the drive to the Jones's house on the edge of King's Barrow was passed in silence. Aromatic silence, but silence nonetheless.

Julia watched the dark, winter landscape passing by outside. Bare fields and bare hedges, just visible in the pools of lights from the street lamps. Her own thoughts were equally as bleak. Not just about Aimiee, although the memory of seeing that skull looking back up at her was bad enough.

Barry was on her mind, too. Surely there must be a connection there. His body was found just a day after they broke ground in the beer garden, where Aimiee's body was lying.

Could Barry have been involved in Aimiee's death? Did someone kill Barry to stop him talking?

After what felt like too short a time, Mark pulled the van up onto the pavement outside his parents' house. It was a sizable, detached property with a bay window and two cars parked on the brickwork driveway. She and Mark had worked late in the bookshop putting the counter together and the street was fairly quiet now, and the main road just a distant drone on the edge of hearing.

Julia held the plastic bag of food in both hands, almost defensively, as they waited for someone to answer Mark's knock on the door.

It was Jones who opened it. His eyes lit up when he saw them, although Julia was pretty sure he was focussed on the food.

"Splendid," he said, leaning out to grab the bag. "Let me take that."

As he leant in, Julia caught the scent of stale beer on the man's breath. It seems that he had taken his earlier advice of having a restoring drink to heart. Perhaps she should have done the same. Maybe the shelves wouldn't have gone up straight but she probably wouldn't be feeling quite so glum if she had.

"What Rhys meant to say was 'lovely to see you both'," Mrs Jones – Sandra – sang out from the hallway, as Julia and Mark stepped inside.

The house was warm and bright. The dining table was laid ready. It should all buck Julia's flagging spirits, but somehow everything was missing the mark.

"I've got some plates warming in the kitchen, I'll just get them," Sandra said, bustling off through the archway, although it was superfluous to tell Julia as it was part of the weekly ritual. "Would you like a drink?"

"Some wine would be great, please," Julia called after her, "if you have it."

Sandra's head popped back through the arch. "Ooh, treating yourself are we?" she asked.

Julia didn't normally trust herself to drink around Mark's parents, but after the day she'd had she felt that she needed one.

Too late, Sandra made the same connection and her face fell. "Sorry, Julia, I didn't mean–" she said.

Jones cut her off by putting a hand on Julia's elbow and guiding her through into the dining room, as Mark followed his mum into the kitchen with the food. "Ignore her. You'll need a drink after today, I expect."

Julia eyed the full pint glass already fizzing away on the dark wood table. "You and me both," she sighed.

Jones just made a humming noise in response. He looked lost in thought. "Yes," he said eventually. The pause had been so long it made Julia jump. "Not nice having all of this business resurface."

"Rhys," Julia said hesitantly, aware of the ire she would draw from Mark and Sandra if they came in and found them discussing the subject. "Do you think Barry could have been involved in Aimiee's death? It's just such a coincidence, what happened to him and then so soon after Aimiee's remains are dug up."

Jones gave her a penetrating look. "Well, I like the way you think because I don't believe in coincidences either, Julia. But Barry was out of the country when Aimiee went missing, and for a week beforehand as well. So I don't think he can have been involved."

"You're certain he was abroad?" Julia blurted out, before she could help herself. It had been a long time ago. The inspector must have a mind like a steel trap to remember that. He'd never demonstrated such prowess of memory on family nights playing partner whist, an activity that usually descended in pretty short order into Mr and Mrs Jones each blaming one another for their poor tricks.

Jones gave half a smile. "Yes," he said. "He was in Ireland on a rugby tour. With me. I remember it well, I had to leave the tour early and fly back to join the investigation."

"Ah," Julia said. That sounded pretty certain.

"I think the club started winning games right after I left. But I'm sure that's just a coincidence," Jones added.

They turned as the door opened and Mark and Sandra came in, each carrying heaped plates of food in both hands.

"And what are you two talking about?" Sandra asked, merrily.

"Rugby," Jones and Julia replied in unison.

Chapter 7

The morning sun reflected off the wet roads. Julia craned sideways in the passenger seat of the van to catch her reflection in the wing mirror. She tutted and scratched away at some of the paint she'd missed with her thumbnail. Sunday had been spent helping Mark with the final touch-ups and somehow she'd got more paint on herself than on the walls. Paint-speckled was probably not the look that Ivan wanted for his front-of-house staff.

Looking at the red streaks on her forehead, her mind was drawn back to her conversation with Charlie.

"Oh, I forgot to say, one of the builders at the pub said that if they get rained off he can come to the shop and give a bit of help. So, pray for rain, I guess." Julia looked up at the black clouds that floated ominously above the moors.

"That's a bit unexpected, isn't it?" Mark asked, eyes fixed on the road ahead as he tucked the van to one side giving a Lycra-clad cyclist the space to pass, just. "Which builder was that?"

"Charlie, I think his name is," Julia said.

"Is he the same one who gave you the heart necklace?" Mark asked.

"I really can't remember who gave me that, I think it was just a joke," Julia said. "And I think Charlie has a thing for Sally, anyway."

"Everyone has a thing for Sally," Mark said grimly.

"What?"

"Sorry, never mind. Anyway, I don't think we need any extra help. It's just a few more shelves now. The difficult part's all done."

"The difficult part?"

"Yeah, the painting. The skilled bit, you know? It's just a bit of grunt work now. Not fussed if he helps or not really."

Looking at the shop before they'd set off in the morning, it didn't seem like the hard part was all out of the way, but Julia refrained from pointing this out.

"Right, here we are." Mark pulled abruptly across the lane and stopped in a spray of gravel in front of the Barley Mow.

Julia shot Mark a glance but he was staring straight ahead and she could tell she wasn't about to get anything more out of him.

She was just about to unbuckle and slide out when she noticed the commotion going on in front of the van.

The builders had made an early start to their week, and were just finishing driving a six-foot metal sign advertising their construction company into the ground at the side of the road.

But it was what was written underneath the company logo that gave Julia pause. 'Meadow Fields Development – Phase I'.

"Phase one?" Julia asked, drawing Mark's attention to the sign. "Where on earth are they planning on putting phase two?"

Mark looked at the sign but only shrugged.

One of the workmen gave the top of the sign a final blow with the sledgehammer he was wielding and turned, hopping down from the ladder he'd been perching on. As he straightened up, Julia recognized the face under the hardhat as Charlie's, who gave her a broad, cheery wave with his free hand.

Julia's hand fluttered up in reply and then she reached for her seat belt. "I'd better shuffle on," she said.

"Hmm," Mark grunted.

Julia slipped down from the van and headed towards the pub.

Inside, she found Ivan pacing behind the bar. He was just hanging up the phone when Julia came in.

"Good morning, Ivan," she called to him.

"Is it?" he asked. His face was scrunched into an unbecoming frown.

"What's the matter?" said Julia, scratching self-consciously at where the paint marks had been.

He shook his head and continued his pacing, like a trapped animal. "It was a mistake letting Rob have the time off. It's nigh on impossible to get anyone in on this notice. I've had to give Helen time and a half."

Julia bit her lip and refrained from pointing out that they were still doing double lunch services.

A thought seemed to strike Ivan and he pivoted suddenly and pointed a finger at her. "That doesn't apply to the front-of-house staff," he said loudly.

Julia held up her hands innocently as she made her way through the parlour. Luckily the diners tipped well. The regular lot, at least, the builders hadn't coughed up much, they seemed to treat the place as a canteen.

* * *

The lunch services were over and the parlour was quiet, save for the noise from the builders that came through off and on. The forensic team had halted their work on the hole they'd been digging, but apparently there were plenty of other nice patches of grass that needed to be dug up, too.

With the builders back outside after their lunch, only Mortimer Watkins propped up the bar, stomping in as usual after birdwatching on the moor. His chunky black binoculars hung around his neck still and a pocketbook of birds sat on the bar in front of him next to his pint of bitter, which he raised before every mouthful and inspected against the light of the window.

He took a sip and replaced the glass. "Not a bad pint," Mortimer said, apparently to Julia as there was no one else present. "What did you say it was?"

"It's the best bitter," Julia replied.

"Hmm." Mortimer nodded thoughtfully. "You pour it very well."

"Um. Thank you," said Julia.

She looked up as the parlour door opened. Rob stepped in and made his way over to the bar, ducking under the low beams. Julia's heart went out as she saw him, he looked pale and there were deep bags under his eyes.

"Hi Rob," she said, her voice gentle. "It's good to see you again."

His eyes flickered up briefly to look at Julia before settling back down on the bar. He drummed distractedly on the wood with his fingers. "I'm here to collect my pay packet," he said by way of reply.

"Right," Julia said, searching in the till for the envelope. Ivan had instructed her to press Rob on when he was coming back to work, but she decided she was going to forget to do that and she slid the pay across the bar for him.

"How are you doing?" Julia asked.

Rob gave a slight shrug. "Fine."

Just then Sally came in from cleaning down the dining room. She greeted Rob with a wave.

Rob looked up at Sally and his eyes widened. He opened his mouth to say something but shut it again, swallowing.

"Are you okay?" Julia asked.

"I said I'm fine!" Rob snapped back. With that, he snatched the pay packet from the bar and hurried back across the flagstones and out of the pub, leaving the door hanging open in his haste.

"What was that about?" Sally asked, gazing out after Rob before pulling the door closed.

"He's really shaken up about what happened to Barry," Julia said.

Sally gave a deep sigh as she came back and rested an elbow on the bar.

"Maybe I should call in on him on the way home. I don't like the thought of him sat in that flat all alone."

"Yeah, good idea," Julia said.

Mortimer swivelled on his stool to face them, his lips smacking as he finished swallowing his beer. "I don't think the lad's living at home at the moment," he said.

"He isn't?" Sally asked.

"No," Mortimer said. "The last few days I've seen him up at his parents' farm. I think he's staying with them."

"Oh," Sally said. "Did you talk to him at all? How is he holding up?"

"No, I didn't talk to him, he was too far away. I was watching him through the binoculars, you see?" Mortimer said.

When Sally gave him a puzzled look, he tapped the black binoculars hanging against his chequered shirt as though in explanation.

Sally stared for a moment longer and then shrugged. "At least he's not on his own, I guess. I'll leave him be," she said, checking for Julia's approval. "Well, I should be getting back to the dining room."

Just as Sally was leaving, a customer came in through the front door. He was a small, wiry man, dressed in an immaculate suit and wearing a pair of glasses with circular black frames. He clutched a dark blue clipboard in both hands.

He stood just inside the door for a second or two, blinking and perhaps letting his eyes adjust to the dim light, before crossing the floor to the bar.

"Is Mr Draisaitl in?" the man asked, standing perfectly upright and addressing Julia.

It took Julia a few moments to realize that he meant Ivan.

"Sure," Julia replied. "I can fetch him. Who shall I say is asking?"

"It's Mr Peabody here. From Biddle Parish Council. I've come about the building works out back."

"Okay," Julia said. "Wait here."

With that she stepped into the low corridor that ran behind the bar and poked her head through into the sweltering kitchen. Ivan was there, standing in the centre of the cramped room, although what he was doing other than getting in the way of Helen's tidying up wasn't obvious to Julia.

"Ivan," Julia said, a little meekly, but loud enough to rise above the clatter of pans and plates.

The landlord looked up irritably from the counter he was inspecting, sweat beaded on his forehead. "What?"

"There's a man here to see you. Someone from the council."

Ivan scowled darkly, put down the pan he was holding, and then came striding through, wiping his hands on his apron. "What does he want?"

"You'll have to ask him," Julia said, following her boss back into the parlour.

Mr Peabody was stood where she'd left him, polishing his glasses which he quickly placed back onto his face as they appeared.

Julia made a gesture towards him. "Ivan, this is—"

"Mr Peabody," the man said, not holding out his hand but instead shifting his clipboard from underneath his arm and into his grasp, ready for use. "I'm here from Biddle Parish Council. About the building work out back."

"Well, what about it?" Ivan demanded, placing both hands on the top of the bar and leaning forward so heavily that the knuckles began to turn white.

"According to what I have heard," Mr Peabody said, "as well as the sign which I see has been erected at the front of your property, you are intending to build homes on the site?"

"That's right," Ivan said.

"I'm afraid I will have to insist you stop. Immediately." Mr Peabody stuck his chin in the air.

"Why?" Ivan demanded. "I have every right to build there."

"Simply untrue," said Mr Peabody. "You need planning approval from the Council." Julia could hear the capitalization on the last word.

"There was an existing structure there. A coach house." Ivan straightened up to his full height, the top of his head from the eyebrows up lost to sight behind the oak beam over the bar. "So I don't need planning permission." The landlord stopped short of adding 'ner-nerna-ner-ner' on the end, but it was implied all the same.

Mr Peabody shook his head and allowed a practised, ironic laugh. "It's an existing structure, but you still need to meet several requirements." He began to rattle them off one by one, counting on his fingers as he went through the list. "Building Regulations; Change of Use; Utilities and Services. The list goes on. The existing structure could have been listed for reasons of historical importance or architectural beauty."

"It really wouldn't have been," Julia chipped in helpfully.

"That's just a load of codswallop," Ivan growled.

Mr Peabody clutched his clipboard protectively, as though the word had stung him. "I assure you it's not. Now there's going to be a special meeting of Biddle Parish Council on Monday evening at the primary school to discuss the matter. I suggest you be there."

Ivan leaned across the bar so that his nose was almost touching Mr Peabody's. "Get out of my pub," he hissed.

Mr Peabody swallowed and his voice went up an octave. But to his credit he remained where he was. "I will leave exactly when I intend to," he said.

Ivan extended a hand, trembling with rage, index finger out pointing towards Mr Peabody's face. "I'm warning you!"

Julia laid a hand gently on Ivan's shaking forearm. "Ivan," she murmured.

The large man exhaled heavily through his nostrils but he allowed his arm to slowly retract.

Mr Peabody nodded with satisfaction and adjusted his glasses. "And now," he said, "I will take my leave. Good day to you both." With that he turned on his heel and walked smartly to the exit.

"That little pipsqueak," Ivan said, staring at the parlour door as it clicked shut. "I'll wring his neck."

"Will you go to the meeting?" Julia asked. Ivan's head swivelled to look at her. There was a vein pulsing on his temple and she instantly regretted speaking.

"No need," Ivan replied, his voice raised to a shout. "I know what I'm doing here. I don't have to."

With that he turned and stalked back through the door. A moment later came the sound of muffled yelling from the kitchen.

* * *

Just before her shift finished, Julia had received a text from Janice Teller asking if she would come up and visit.

Ominous, Julia thought. Undoubtedly, Jones had been up to question them with his usual direct manner and it wouldn't surprise Julia in the least if he'd let slip that she was the one who set him on their trail.

So now she found herself trudging up the lane towards the Tellers' cottage. By rights she should have been at the shop helping Mark, but after setting his dad onto Janice, it seemed that going to check she was okay was the least that she could do.

The black clouds had swept right on overhead without a drop of rain falling and the now the sun, sitting low on the horizon, bathed the lane and the hedgerows in a cold, ruby light.

From Forge's Lane, Julia descended down the steep, rutted track towards the old forge, now the Tellers' home. In front of her, the village of Biddle Rhyne lay at the foot of the hill, at this distance looking sleepy and serene in the last of the sunlight. Although, of course, it was usually sleepy and serene up close as well.

Julia opened the wooden gate and let herself into the patioed front garden of the cottage. Lance had lovingly and almost single-handedly restored it from the tumbledown wreck it had been and now, even in the dead of winter, it looked absolutely picturesque. All it lacked was a curl of smoke from the chimney and it could easily have been in a painting.

As she crossed the patio, Julia walked past person-height stacks of pots. The ceramic work, present in all shapes and sizes, was the output of Lance's industry. The man definitely had a talent with his hands.

Julia hovered with her hand over the heavy iron knocker. Yes, Janice had invited her up here, but she was still rather unnerved at the prospect of Lance answering the door. The last time she'd been at the cottage, he'd really given her both barrels. Perhaps he'd done so deservedly, she had been snooping around. But even so the image of the hulking man shouting and raving at her had left her deeply wary of Lance.

There was a click and the door was flung open, leaving Julia with her hand hanging in the empty air. It seemed that her approach up the lane hadn't gone unobserved.

To her relief it was Janice who stood now before her. She looked different from how Julia remembered. She'd always been thin, with striking cheekbones. But now she looked paler, almost gaunt, and her flowing blonde hair had been chopped into a short bob that finished just before her shoulders.

She gave a welcoming smile, but all the same she looked tense and uneasy. The police had probably interrogated her the day before, Julia reminded herself, and DI Jones could be rather an intimidating figure when he chose to be.

"Come in, come in." Janice beckoned and stepped aside to allow Julia in.

Julia's eyes quickly adjusted to the dim light which was all the little period windows allowed through; all the electric lights overhead were off. It was the first time Julia had been inside the cottage but it was every bit as neat and well-kept as the outside, with many of the fixtures apparently authentic to the building's period. It certainly hadn't been a cheap refit.

Julia glanced through the open doors to the kitchen and the sitting room. "Is Lance about?" she asked.

Janice gave a mirthless, dry laugh. "He's gone," she said. "When I told him about me and Barry he didn't bother sticking around."

Julia's eyes widened. "He left you?" she gasped.

"Yes. He left me with a huge pile of debt and an even higher pile of pots that no one wants to buy. You don't need any, do you?"

"I... I..." Julia stammered.

Janice touched her gently on the arm. "I was only teasing you, love."

Julia did her best to laugh, but she couldn't find anything funny about the situation. It was no secret that the garden centre had only paid such high premiums for Lance's work because he had been sleeping for some time with Mrs White. And for him to abandon Janice over one night's affair with Barry? The hypocrisy of it was breathtaking.

"I can't believe he just walked out on you like that," Julia said.

Janice shrugged. "But he did. I'll tell you what I told that personable police inspector who came by yesterday. I haven't seen Lance in weeks. If he's anywhere near Biddle Rhyne then it's news to me. If anyone does see him then I have some bills with his name on them."

Jones would be trying to track him down, Julia thought. For his own sake she hoped that Lance had an alibi for wherever he was, though, because it certainly didn't sound like he'd been ready to bury the hatchet with poor Barry.

"I'm sorry I told the inspector about you and Barry," Julia said.

"That's okay, I understand," Janice said as she guided Julia on through to the small sitting room that looked out over the hillside.

Julia shivered slightly as she sat down. It was cold in the house, as well as dark. She realized that Janice must have been saving every penny she could.

"I thought you'd brought me here to have a go at me," Julia admitted.

"On the contrary, I wanted to check you were okay," Janice said softly, taking a seat on the sofa.

"Me? But you're the one—" Julia cut herself short and looked abashed at the carpet.

Janice waved it away. "Yes, yes. I know all about my own troubles. They're nothing really. I harboured Barry no ill will, I'm sure the police will come to see that. And I've been abandoned by my husband, but I'm probably better off without him. But you? Finding Barry like that? That can't have been pleasant."

Julia wasn't sure how to answer so she stayed silent.

Janice lifted a packet of cigarettes from the coffee table. "You don't mind, do you?" she asked, lighting one as Julia shook her head.

"You knew Barry as well," Julia said.

Janice gave a bark of laughter that made Julia jump. "That's one way to put it."

"Did he mention anyone else who might have wanted to hurt him?"

Janice shook her head. "Sorry. Barry and I were really not that intimate with one another. If he had any concerns, I don't think he'd have been sharing them with me." She blew cigarette smoke out and it drifted up to the low ceiling.

Julia's phone buzzed and she pulled it from her handbag. "It's Mark seeing where I've got to. I'm meant to be helping him paint," she said apologetically.

Janice waved her cigarette at Julia. "It's fine, you go."

Julia stood. "Take care of yourself. If you ever want to pop into the Barley Mow then maybe I could get you some drinks on the house."

Janice grinned. "Why, is Ivan no longer running the place?"

Julia laughed.

"Don't worry about me, Julia, I'm not a charity case. Not yet anyway. You go, I'll be fine."

Julia paused on her way to the door. "Janice?" she asked.

"Yes?" The other woman hadn't moved from her seat.

"You were in Aimiee's year at school, weren't you? Do you remember anything from when she disappeared? Anyone that was suspicious at the time?"

Janice looked taken aback and took some time to answer, the cigarette hanging limp and forgotten in her fingers. Finally, she pulled herself together and took a drag before replying, ash spilling onto the arm of the sofa.

"No," Janice said shortly. "Nothing. The police didn't have any leads. I think she just vanished."

Before Julia could reply, Janice waved a hand towards the door. "Anyway, you said you needed to be going. Don't let me keep you. Like I said I'll be fine."

Julia cast a glance back into the cottage as she let herself out. It was hard to tell in the gloomy light, but she was sure the colour had drained from Janice's cheeks.

* * *

67

Radio 2 blared out of Mark's radio, turned up loud to be heard over the sound of the drill.

Teetering on a step ladder, Julia held the shelf steady as Mark worked the screws into the wall, grunting with the effort of getting through the thick masonry. The drill whined in protest and specks of brick dust floated through the air, making Julia's eyes sting. Relative quiet fell as the screw finally bedded itself in.

"I said, excuse me there," a voice announced behind them.

Julia jumped, wobbling on the ladder. She turned to see who had spoken and the shelf, only secured on one side, came down heavily on her shoulder. She swore quietly and grabbed it with one hand, twisting awkwardly to see who their visitor was.

She recognized the slender form of Mr Peabody, standing perfectly in the middle of the room, his clipboard held in front of him in both hands. His lip twitched in what might be a smile.

"I did knock," Mr Peabody said. "But I don't think you heard me over the music." He turned his head meaningfully at the radio by Mark's feet. "You should probably check the decibel level on that. It is after 6 p.m., you know?"

Mark came down off his own step ladder and stooped to flick the radio off. Silence rang out through the shop.

"Who are you, sorry?" Mark said.

Mr Peabody's face twitched again. "I'm Mr Peabody. I'm from the Biddle Parish Council's planning inspectorate." He extended a hand out towards Mark.

Warily, Mark shook the man's hand. "And what can we do for you, Inspector?" Mark asked dryly.

"No need to call me 'Inspector'," Mr Peabody replied. Julia saw him stealthily wipe the palm of his hand on his handkerchief. "My proper title would be 'Planning Inspector', anyway, but 'Mr Peabody' will suffice."

"Then, what can I do for you, Mr Peabody?"

"Well. I've just come to check that everything here is in order, vis-à-vis the conversion of the premises into a commercial unit," Mr Peabody said, looking around the room meaningfully and glancing down sporadically at his clipboard.

"All the applications for the change of use were approved," Mark said. "And we're not making any structural changes, nothing that would need planning permission."

"Hm," Mr Peabody said thoughtfully, still looking hither and thither. "The thing is, sometimes what people put on the forms and what they actually do can be different, you see?"

"I can assure you that what we're doing is exactly what we said we would," Julia said.

Mr Peabody nodded. "And this is becoming a bookshop, is that correct?"

"No," Mark said. "We're going to sell turnips."

Mr Peabody's brow furrowed. "Turnips? Interesting." He pulled the pen from the top of the clipboard and clicked the nib out.

Julia glared at Mark but he didn't seem to notice. She didn't think Mark quite realized who they were dealing with. "My ever-amusing boyfriend is joking, Mr Peabody. This is going to be a bookshop."

Mr Peabody looked up at Julia and clicked the pen away again. "I see. Very droll, Mr Jones. And do you still think you're on course to open at the start of next month? I understand this was a stipulation of you taking ownership of the unit."

"We should be on course," Mark said, casting an eye over his handiwork. "Assuming we don't have too many interruptions."

If Mr Peabody caught Mark's drift then he didn't show it, but he scribbled something down on his clipboard before continuing. "And one thing I did want to check is the fire-exit situation."

Now it was Julia's turn to frown. She pointed over her shoulder at the fire door. With some effort she managed to keep her tone level. "Like Mr Jones said, we haven't changed anything structural. The fire exit is still there, just as before."

"Good, good," Mr Peabody said. He drifted behind the counter towards the fire exit in question and examined it closely. Mark's toolbox lay just in front of it and Mr Peabody studied that, too, jotting something down.

As Julia and Mark exchanged glances behind his back, Mr Peabody finished writing and spoke. "I just wanted to check, as, due to the nature of the new premises, fire exits would be a paramount concern."

"Nature of the premises?" Julia asked.

Mr Peabody turned back to them and nodded. "Namely, being a bookshop."

Julia looked at him confused, so he carried on, his tone weary. "Books are highly flammable, you see, Miss Ford? And so I wanted to check if the fire exits were adequate given the change in use of the building."

"But it used to be a library," said Julia.

"I don't see how that's relevant," Mr Peabody said.

"The library had lots of books. More than our shop will," Julia said.

"Miss Ford," Mr Peabody said. "I'm not concerned with what the building used to be, I'm concerned with the here and now. And the immediate future."

Mark made a small, strangled noise in the back of his throat. Julia looked at him and could see his jaw clenching and unclenching. "Mr Peabody," he said, a slight growl in his voice. "If you're quite done here, we have work to do. Perhaps I could ask you to leave? Through whichever exit suits you the best."

Mr Peabody lowered his clipboard and looked Mark in the eye. "There was no need to be rude, Mr Jones," he said. "No need at all."

With a parting look, Mr Peabody strode from the room, leaving by the main door.

Chapter 8

Julia was in work early the next morning to prepare for the lunch rush. But after the tables were all laid there was little enough to do but loiter behind the bar and wait, although she knew the kitchen was a hive of activity. A couple of ramblers came in shortly after the doors opened and sat warming themselves by the fire, drinking coffees, but it still left Julia a lot of time for her thoughts.

She was convinced that Janice didn't have it in her to kill Barry. And although she would privately admit her suspicion that Lance might be capable, he would be displaying a level of guile he normally didn't by sneaking around unseen. Perhaps he'd returned to Biddle Rhyne in the unidentified Micra? But would he have been able to talk his way into Barry's house? Julia didn't think he could keep a lid on his temper for long enough.

Her thoughts circled round again to Janice and her cold, lonesome cottage. Living like that could harden someone.

Ivan came in from the back, a stack of menus in his hand. No matter how quiet the pub was, the landlord always seemed to be busy.

"Ivan," Julia called to him as she passed. "I've been thinking."

"Not what I pay you for," Ivan said, squeezing past her without stopping.

Julia trailed after him undeterred, "I was thinking that maybe we could get some plants or something for the garden."

"I'm not much of a gardener," Ivan said as he deposited the menus in the dining room and went back the way he'd come.

"I know Janice Teller has some nice pots going cheap," Julia called after him.

If the thought of a bargain didn't tempt him, then nothing would, but Ivan just disappeared into the back corridor again, the sound of his heavy footsteps receding in the direction of the cellar.

Julia sighed and resumed her position at the bar.

Just after half eleven, the outside door opened and Detective Inspector Jones stepped inside. He stood for a moment, taking in the mostly empty room before crossing across the worn flagstone floor, stooping his tall frame to get under the blackened oak beams.

In spite of the frosty weather outside, he still didn't wear a coat. He was in his civvies rather than dressed for work: faded blue jeans strapped a little too tight against his wide girth with a brown leather belt and a chequered button-down shirt that was tucked in at the waist, a woolly cardy over the top. His only concession to the cold weather outside appeared to be the Oddballs Rugby hat perched on top of his head.

In spite of her best efforts to the contrary, Julia saw him fairly often at family gatherings, but she never got used to seeing him in his civilian clothes. Somehow he always seemed much better suited to his formal work wear, despite the fact he'd never taken the time to find a single suit that fitted properly.

Jones greeted Julia as he arrived at the bar, pulling his hat from his head and stuffing it into a back pocket of his jeans. At that moment Ivan appeared again from the doorway behind the bar and Jones raised a large hand in salutation.

"Rhys, hello," Ivan said, extending a hand between the sets of pumps on the bar.

Jones shook it and then settled heavily onto one of the stools. "Hello, Ivan," he returned.

Julia hadn't realized the two men knew each other, although the fact was hardly surprising, they had both lived in the area since well before she was born.

"I'm sorry about your Barry," Jones said, shaking his head. "Really nasty bit of business."

Ivan prodded at a bar mat that had come slightly askew and bit his bottom lip. "Yes, it was," he replied. "Have you got some questions for me?"

"No, no, nothing like that," Jones replied. "This is just a social call, that's all. And maybe an excuse for an early lunch. All this made me realize that it was a long time since I'd stuck my head in."

"Right, right," Ivan said, seeming to relax a little and leaning one elbow on the bar. "You knew Barry a bit, if I recall correctly."

"Only as a kid," Jones said. "I coached him one year."

"Oh, that's right," Ivan said. "You were the Under-18s coach. So I guess that made Barry seventeen, then."

"Sixteen, actually," Jones corrected him. "He played up an age group. Talented lad he was."

"Of course. You had him playing at loosehead and his brother at tighthead. Those two caused some damage, didn't they?"

"Usually to each other," Jones said and the two men erupted into rumbles of laughter, although it was all a bit lost on Julia.

"Oh, those were some good times when the two of them were playing," Jones said, staring dreamy eyed at the brass decorations that were hung over the bar.

"They weren't for me," Ivan said, although his tone was still light-hearted. "Terrence was meant to be here washing up but he was always missing his shifts either because he was playing rugby or training for playing rugby. Or injured from playing rugby."

"I had forgotten that Terrence worked here," said Jones.

"So did Terrence, that was the problem," said Ivan.

The two men laughed again and then lapsed into silence.

"I didn't know Barry used to play rugby," Julia said. It was funny that she'd worked alongside him for years and he'd never mentioned it.

Jones gave a small smile. "Oh, yes, quite the athlete, Barry was. Strong, motivated."

This wasn't an entirely accurate description of the Barry that Julia had known. Whether they were eulogizing him or whether he'd had an abrupt personality shift since he was a teenager, she wasn't sure.

The two men were silent for a moment, apparently lost in thought, and then Ivan slammed a palm on the bar. "Anyway. What can I get for you, Inspector?"

Jones scratched at his moustache and looked at the chalkboards fixed to the wall. "I think, a cup of black coffee and, oh, maybe a Spotted Dick, too," he said. "I'll eat here at the bar if that's all right?"

"No problem. Frees a table up, anyway," Ivan said. Well, that was unexpected, usually the landlord was strictly against food in the parlour. Evidently he had a soft spot for the inspector.

Ivan turned to Julia. "Can you get the coffee? I'll take that order through to the kitchen."

"Of course," Julia said, and reached under the counter for a cup as Ivan bustled back the way he'd come. She caught Jones's eye as she straightened up.

"What's that look for?" Jones asked.

"Nothing, nothing," Julia said.

"Now, come on, out with it."

"Spotted Dick? I thought this was meant to be your lunch."

The policeman's countenance darkened. "What of it? I've got my major food groups covered. I've got spotted. I've got dick."

Julia didn't say anything but turned to start work on the coffee machine which took up a good chunk of the counter behind the bar.

"Don't say anything to Sandra."

Julia smiled and spoke back over her shoulder, raising her voice over the noise of the steam. "Don't worry, I won't."

"Or Mark," Jones said after a pause. "You know what a gossip the lad is."

Julia wiped down the spout of the machine and placed the drink in front of the policeman. "Your secret's safe with me," she said.

"I hope so," Jones mumbled.

"How is the investigation going?" Julia asked, leaning against the bar and watching Jones as he emptied sugar into his coffee and gave it a vigorous stir.

"It's going fine," he replied tersely.

"Are you still looking for Lance?" asked Julia.

"I still need to talk to him, yes," Jones said.

"I'll keep an eye out for him," said Julia.

Jones stopped stirring and pointed the teaspoon in Julia's direction. "Listen to me, Julia," he said. "I don't want you poking your nose into this. It's a police investigation. Do you understand?"

"Yes," Julia said. She was still going to keep an eye out for Lance.

* * *

As Julia stepped out into the car park, the sun just dipping below the horizon, she was a bit surprised to hear the rapid clatter of paws on the gravel shortly followed by a brown Labrador crashing into her shins.

She wobbled to recover her balance and saw a wagging tail disappearing back the way it had come.

"Manny?" she asked.

Upon hearing its name, the dog gave another woof, turned clumsily and came bounding back again to Julia. It was definitely Mark's dog, but she hadn't been expecting Mark to meet her, and anyway, she couldn't spot him.

Full of boundless energy, as he normally was, Manny sped away again, this time darting around the corner of the pub. Julia followed, somewhat less energetically, and saw Mark leaning on the fence that separated the Barley Mow from the fields. He seemed to be staring, riveted, at the construction work going on in the beer garden, which was just rounding up for the day, the workers beginning to trail in towards the pub.

Julia frowned as she made her way down the side of the building towards him. He seemed to be looking at the builders making their way inside. She couldn't help but wonder if he was looking out for Charlie. She'd never pegged him as the jealous type.

"Hello," Julia called to him as she approached.

He turned, apparently only noticing her for the first time, and gave her a quick peck on the cheek as she arrived. Manny crashed past, squeezing under a surprisingly small gap in the fence and disappearing off into the long grass of the field on the other side.

"I wasn't expecting you to pick me up," Julia said as they started heading towards Mark's van, parked up near the entrance.

Mark shrugged. "I just thought it would be nice to see you. I needed a bit of a break at the shop, to be honest."

"Do I allow you breaks?" Julia teased.

"Don't worry, I'm making good progress. Ahead of schedule, if anything."

Mark sounded solemn, it was hard to tell if he had registered that Julia was joking or not, but before she could reply Manny came thundering back from the fields. "Come on, you mutt," Mark sighed, and opened the van door.

With a last, longing look, Manny turned and jumped up into the van and Julia followed him in.

"Are we still working on the shop tonight?" Julia asked.

Mark turned the key, and the van juddered into life. "Sure," he said. "There's always plenty to do."

He guided the van out towards the lane but as he reached the car park exit a car shot past, engine revving. Mark swore and pumped the brakes hard, sending Julia and Manny jolting forwards.

"The drivers around here, honestly," Mark said.

"Mark!" Julia said, squeaking with excitement.

"I wouldn't have hit them, I had plenty of space," Mark said.

Julia smacked a palm against his shoulder repeatedly. "Mark!" she said again.

"What?"

Julia flapped a hand in the direction the car had gone. "That was our white Micra!"

Mark's lips pursed into a little o-shape and he threw the van into gear, hauling it onto the lane and accelerating sharply.

"Are you sure it's the same one?" he asked, eyes glued to the road.

"I think I recognized a dent in the bumper," Julia said.

As they rounded the bend, they could just see the small white car up ahead. It had passed the turn off for the high street and was heading up the steep slope of Pagan's Hill.

Julia's mouth curled into a quiet smile of satisfaction. There was no way through up there, they wouldn't get away.

She urged Mark on all the same. "Get closer, see if we can get their plates."

Mark put his foot down and the lane sped by.

"But not too fast," Julia said, clutching the seat.

Mark ignored this and pressed on, but the van struggled on the steep incline and the car increased the gap then disappeared around the next corner. By the time they rounded the bend it had gone, whether up one of the turnings or further on round the next corner it wasn't obvious.

Julia peered down the sporadic tracks and side roads that spurred off the lane, but didn't spot anything and they carried on up the hill.

Finally, they reached the end of the road, near the top of the hill. The little gravel parking area was empty.

"He must have snuck off down one of the side roads," Julia said.

"Yes," Mark agreed, tugging hard on the steering wheel to turn the van in the narrow space, gravel crunching under the wheels. "Keep your eyes peeled."

The van started on its way back down the hill, but they hadn't made it far when Julia's heart sank.

"Look," she said, pointing.

Mark's eyes flickered up from the road. A little further down the hill, rising smoke was visible through the sparse trees.

"Too much to hope it's a bonfire, I suppose," he said, easing off the brake to quicken their approach.

The smoke was coming from one of the small farm tracks part way down the hill. By the time they reached the turn-off – what felt like only a moment later – the smoke had thickened into ugly black clouds that curled away over the village.

The van bumped down the rutted track, and as it turned a corner the fire came into view. Orange and red flames leapt skyward, within them Julia could just make out the charred black outline of the car, already reduced to a twisted black hulk.

Mark brought the van to a halt a few feet away and they stepped out.

Even from that distance the heat coming off the burning car was intense.

"I can't see anyone inside," Mark said, shielding his eyes but doing his best to look into the flames.

"No, I don't think so," Julia said. Not that she could tell for certain but there didn't seem to be anyone. She looked around for signs of the driver. If he'd run into the woods and kept his head down, they'd have no chance of spotting him.

After panning across the treeline she glanced downhill and squinted. "There!" she shouted.

Running through the fields she could just make out a man charging away towards the village. He'd already made a pretty good distance away from them.

Mark strode back to the van and opened the door. Manny uncoiled from the seat and landed at his feet.

Mark pointed at the receding figure in the fields. "After him, Manny," he commanded.

The dog barked excitedly and jumped up, putting his paws on Mark's stomach.

Mark shoved him down, pointed again at the fields. "That way. Fetch!"

Manny let out another woof and raced off, paws scrabbling, speeding in the other direction, up the hill and into his favourite woodlands.

Mark looked from the dog and then down to the fleeing figure, now disappearing behind the shoulder of the hill.

"I don't think we're catching him," he muttered.

Julia watched him run out of sight and then looked back to the blazing car. Any chance of getting the plates were quickly being reduced to ashes. "I'll call the fire brigade," Julia sighed.

Chapter 9

Julia ran the vacuum cleaner around the bookshop floor, the noise drowning out the sound of the morning rush hour outside on the high street.

It had been a hard morning's work, but the shelves were now all in place. After she and Mark had finished the ordeal of putting up the wall-mounted ones, the free-standing shelves had sprung up in what seemed like moments. Already it looked like a shop, even with all of the shelves empty, which made Julia's heart flutter. She felt a definite spring in her step.

But somehow, defying all Julia's understanding of physics, when they'd drawn the dust sheets back it had revealed a carpet thick with flecks of the previous coat of paint which they'd stripped off as well as dozens upon dozens of splinters of wood from the earlier carpentry.

Still, the industrial-strength vacuum that Mark had brought in was making short work of it, and almost half the carpet was back to something resembling its original state now.

As she worked, a hay bale went past the window, catching Julia's eye, soon after followed by a large red tractor and then a trailer stacked high with further bales. A second tractor trundled by, then a third. Like the first, they both had a hay bale skewered on its hay fork and trailers full to overflowing at the rear. Two more tractors followed on and after that there was the long, inevitable string of cars, each with its own irate driver, late for work.

Julia stood pondering the slow-moving convoy and feeling sorry for the commuters before it finally dawned on her that she, too, would get stuck in the same traffic jam on the way to the Barley Mow. Sally was meant to be picking her up soon and by the looks of it she would be travelling down the high street at all of ten miles an hour.

Julia realized that Sally should be there any moment now, traffic notwithstanding, so she dusted herself down and handed the vacuum over to Mark before collecting her handbag and going to wait at the front door.

She sat on the step, enjoying the morning air as the cars crawled by. Eventually, one of the cars in the line of traffic peeled away and Sally pulled up, looking decidedly unamused.

"The traffic's just awful. There must have been an accident or something," Sally said as Julia climbed into the passenger seat and belted up.

"There was a load of tractors up ahead carting hay bales about," said Julia.

Sally scowled as she nosed her way back out into the stream of traffic, leaving the driver behind little choice in the matter.

They didn't get far, barely three hundred yards, before they came to a halt. Nothing seemed to be coming in the other direction either. To add insult to injury, a handful of strands of hay floated down on the morning breeze and arranged themselves over Sally's windscreen.

"What idiot moves hay bales about in the middle of rush hour?" Sally asked.

Her question was answered some time later when they pulled into the Barley Mow, where Ivan was signing off receipt for the delivery on a clipboard.

As Ivan handed the paperwork back to one of the farmers, he gave the two women a broad, cheery wave.

"Ivan, what on earth is going on here?" Julia asked, stepping out of the car and gazing up in wonder.

Already there were thirty or so hay bales stacked like bricks forming a wall on the patch of grass at the edge of the car park that ran alongside the road. Two of the tractors were hard at work, using the hay forks on their fronts to skewer bales off the trailers and raise them up, placing them ponderously on the top of the wall.

The landlord looked up at the mound of bales with an expression of proprietorial satisfaction. "It's a kind of advertisement. A new spin on the pub sign." When he saw Julia and Sally looking puzzled at him he carried on. "It's a barley mow, get it?"

"But it's not barley, it's hay," Sally pointed out.

"Never mind that," said Ivan, "no one knows the difference anyway."

"I knew." Sally sniffed.

Ivan ignored her and waved his hands dramatically at the stack. "People are going to see it and think 'Barley Mow'."

Julia bit her lip and continued to gaze as the pile of hay increased in size. It would certainly be hard to miss. But then there was no other building within a quarter of a mile anyway. The giant, sprawling coaching inn stood out in the flat landscape already. So far the old, traditional sign had never let them down.

Ivan glanced at his watch. "Anyway, girls, you'd better hurry on in, you're late for work."

"There was bad traffic on the high street," Sally observed darkly.

The nearest farmer had the good grace to look sheepish, but if Ivan caught Sally's meaning then he didn't let on. "Go on, before I dock your wages," he said.

Julia and Sally turned their back on the industrious tractors and headed for the pub. "Ivan's up to something," Julia whispered as they walked.

"No change there, I guess," Sally replied.

* * *

Julia deposited the stack of dirty plates into the sink and straightened up, easing a knot out of her spine.

"I might take my break now, Ivan, okay?" she called across the kitchen.

"Nope," Ivan responded without looking up from his work.

Julia was just pulling her apron off to go when Ivan glanced up at her. "I mean it. There's a delivery out back you need to take care of."

Julia frowned at the landlord. "Delivery?"

Taking deliveries had never been part of her job but the man was obviously enjoying her confusion so she just rolled her eyes and headed out through the kitchen door to the back of the building.

It had better not be more hay, Julia thought.

When she emerged outside she found a white transit was sat idling on the gravel. Julia was still none the wiser until the driver, a burly middle-aged man, hopped down and slid the side door open. Just inside the van was a stack of four huge ceramic pots.

Julia's heart melted. So Ivan had ordered them after all.

"Where do you want them?" the driver asked, looking past Julia's shoulder at the rough wooden fence that housed the pub's many and varied rubbish bins.

Julia pointed instead through the narrow gate that led to the beer garden. "Just there by the picnic tables, please."

The man tutted, as though she'd personally picked the location to make his day harder, but all the same he retrieved a wheeled dolly from inside the van.

As he did so, Julia inspected the pots and ran her fingers over the rough material. They were sturdy and circled with intriguing, waving patterns, no two exactly alike. Say what you like about Lance Teller, the man did know his craft.

She stood aside as the van's driver hauled them down, grunting with the effort, and strapped them to the dolly, then she ran a few paces ahead to hold the gate for him, squeezing to one side as he navigated through.

"Well, do you like them?" Ivan appeared behind her making Julia start. For such a big man, he managed to sneak around when it pleased him.

"Yes," Julia said, doing her best to look pleased and not startled.

"I decided that maybe the old garden could use a bit of sprucing up after all. Pardon the pun!" Ivan's face split ear to ear in a grin as he reached through the open doorway into the pub and retrieved four tiny spruce trees, grasping two in each hand just above the roots.

Each tree had a tiny ball of earth around the roots, little more than the size of a cricket ball. Julia glanced quickly from the diminutive trees to the goliath sized pots that the wheezing man was just finishing unloading onto the paving stones.

"Oh dear," Julia said. "I think I'm going to need to ask Mark to get some topsoil when he's next at the garden centre. Lots of topsoil, in fact."

Ivan pulled a face at her. "Think, girl, think. We've got a literal mound of the stuff over there." He waved a meaty hand in the direction of the pile the builders had hauled out of the ground in the previous days.

"Right," Julia said.

Ivan gestured in the direction of the bin store. "There's a wheelbarrow in there, I think," he said. "It's been a while since anyone used it, but it should still be there. Help yourself to it."

With that he turned and headed back inside, a spring in his step.

Julia watched him go. "Thanks," she said.

Waving goodbye to the driver, she pulled the bolt back on the bin store and peered inside, wondering if this gardening counted towards her hours or not.

* * *

That afternoon the heavens opened. After watching the builders lounge around the parlour being paid to do very little, Ivan had cut his losses and dismissed them for the day. The sound of rain drumming on the roof of the pub continued relentlessly all the way into the evening.

Ivan stood at the parlour window, legs planted wide apart, arms folded, watching the downpour on the other side of the pane with a scowl etched onto his face. Julia and Sally exchanged nervous glances and tiptoed around their boss.

Eventually, just before ten, the last of the customers bade them goodnight and scurried from the door towards their car, their coats hoisted over their heads in an attempt to keep off the worst of the storm.

While Sally pretended to be busy behind the bar, Julia walked softly up to Ivan.

"Never mind," she said. "I'm sure they said it's meant to be dry tomorrow. Maybe they'll make up for some of the lost time."

"I doubt it," said Ivan, blackly. "Did you ever see such a shiftless lot? They'll milk me for every penny I'm worth."

Julia tutted in reproach. "They're not that bad, Ivan," she said.

The landlord let out a deep sigh. "It's not just the cost," he explained, "although goodness knows that's bad enough."

Julia braced herself. If there was something troubling Ivan more than money then it must be dire.

"It's that pencil pusher from the council sniffing around here," Ivan said. "The more progress I've made the more likely it is for the council just to wave it all through. If all I've got is a sodden hole in the ground, there's a high chance they'll just order me to fill it in again, and then where will I be?"

Julia didn't reply. She wasn't sure she believed the truth in that. She wasn't even sure Ivan did. It seemed that for all his bluster he'd known deep down that he needed some sort of permission to build on the site, old coach house or no old coach house. It was hard to tell with him sometimes where his bravado ended and sincerity began.

Ivan turned finally from his vigil at the window and seemed surprised to find the pub empty and the fire burning low in the grate.

"You two might as well be off," Ivan said. "If anyone does turn up to squeeze one in before last orders, I'm sure I can manage it." He shot a last filthy glance at the rain coming down outside. "Somehow I doubt it, though."

Julia and Sally mumbled their thanks and quickly went to snatch their coats from the hooks before he changed his mind.

Julia just had her hand upon the latch when Ivan spoke again. "You know what?" he said.

Julia held her breath.

"If there are any more punters then screw 'em. It's their own silly fault for being abroad on a night like this."

Sally and Julia laughed and stepped over the threshold. The parlour door shut behind them and they heard the sound of the heavy deadbolt sliding into place.

The two of them stood pressed against the wooden door for a moment, the empty pub providing shelter against the worst of the driving rain, as they summoned their courage to sprint around to the side car park.

Sally struggled to unfold an umbrella against the howling wind, eventually managing to hold it somewhat steady by using both hands. She looked over to Julia. "Ready?" she asked.

Julia nodded and the two of them ran, huddled together and giggling under the single umbrella following the wall of the building through the darkened car park.

Just as they rounded the corner, Julia realized that they weren't alone.

A shadow unpeeled itself from the side of the towering haystack by the side of the road and stepped out onto the car park.

At first Julia thought it was just her eyes playing tricks on her, some hay blowing loose that looked like a person. She wiped the rainwater from her face with her hand. But there was definitely a man there, coming towards them – a tall figure, dressed head to toe in black, with their hood pulled up and a scarf covering his face.

Julia let out a scream, almost drowned out entirely by the howl of the wind and the pelting of raindrops on the ground, but it was enough to draw Sally's attention and she saw her friend's head snap round.

"Come on," Sally urged, raising her voice to be heard, and Julia felt a persistent tug at her arm as her friend pulled her on faster towards their car.

The figure gave chase, gaining speed as he sprinted towards them, easily closing the distance.

They reached the car and instinctively Julia grabbed the handle and wrenched at it, but of course the car was locked.

Sally let the umbrella fall to the floor and delved into her pocket for her keys, her soaked fingers fumbling them as she drew them out and they bounced from the side of the car, landing somewhere on the dark ground.

Julia saw Sally drop to her knees, scrabbling desperately in the gravel for the keys and she hurried around the car to help, fingers probing hopelessly in the blackness and coming up empty.

The sound of the chasing footfalls were closer now, terribly close. Julia looked up and saw the black figure almost upon them, looming tall. She began to rise, holding both hands out defensively.

The man reached them. One long arm flashed out towards her and Julia screamed. His hand connected roughly with her shoulder, knocking her backwards, and the ground rose up to meet her, the sharp rocks biting her painfully as she landed.

She kicked about trying to stand, but in her panic her footing slipped on the loose stones and she only managed to climb to her knees.

Helpless, she saw the man barrel past her to Sally and could only watch in horror as he reached an arm down towards her neck. At first Julia thought he was about to try and throttle her, but instead he snatched at her necklace, his fist closing firmly around the chain before violently pulling away.

A gasp escaped Sally's lips as the old clasp broke and the necklace came streaming free. Clutching his prize, their assailant turned and began racing away towards the lane.

Within an instant, Sally grabbed up the fallen umbrella by the end and was on her feet chasing after him, brandishing the solid wooden handle menacingly in the air.

"Don't, Sally!" Julia pleaded, holding her grazed palm out towards her.

But it was no use. Sally thundered on, umbrella waving. "Give me my pendant back, you dullard!" she screamed.

The figure increased his pace, sprinting off through the rain onto the street, and disappeared into the night.

Sally came skidding to a halt and thrust the umbrella in his direction. "You'd better run!" she shouted into the darkness.

Julia had managed to catch her footing, and her breath, and made her way quickly to join her friend, laying a hand on her shoulder.

Sally spun, umbrella raised and ready to strike.

"Sally, it's me!" Julia yelled.

Sally stopped herself just in time, and instead enveloped Julia in a hug. They stood for a moment, both shaking and soaked through to the bone.

Julia pulled herself free and stepped back. "We should get out of here, there's no knowing if he'll be back. Let's find the keys."

* * *

Sally shoved her foot down on the accelerator as they left the car park; the engine roared and gravel sprayed back from the wheels, but she mishandled the gearstick terribly and the car jolted slowly along the lane.

On her second attempt she slid the car into gear and they accelerated away through the puddles.

"I can't see a thing in this rain," Sally muttered, leaning forward to the windscreen.

"Headlights," Julia prompted.

Sally turned the car lights on, although it did little to help; the road was still hidden in the downpour. Sally slowed a little.

Julia couldn't help herself from peering out at the passing hedgerow, searching for a figure lurking there. She could feel her whole body shaking still as the adrenaline percolated through her system.

"I'm going to call Mark," Julia said. "I think I could do with him staying over tonight."

"Good idea."

Julia groped around in her bag for her phone. She glared at the screen. The world seemed to be conspiring against her that night. "I've got no signal," she said.

"Use my phone if you like," Sally said. "It's in the glovebox."

Julia popped it open and pulled out the Galaxy, using her finger to draw the little squiggle which unlocked it. She paused. "Do you have Mark's number on here?" she asked.

"Of course."

Julia scrolled down to find it, but the call went straight to answerphone.

"I can stop by the bookshop if you like. He might still be working there," Sally suggested.

Julia glanced at the clock on the dash. "Worth a try," she said. She took a deep breath as she tried to calm down. "You shouldn't have gone after him like that, Sally, it was dangerous."

Sally shrugged and splashed on through the overflowing gutters. "But Charlie gave it to me," she said.

Julia made a show of rolling her eyes but inwardly she rather admired Sally's willingness to defend what was hers. "You never know, maybe the police will find it," she said.

Sally snorted. "Unlikely."

They reached the bookshop but the building, like the rest of the street, was dark and Mark's van was nowhere to be seen.

"I guess he's already in bed then," Sally said.

It was a little early for Mark to be in bed, Julia judged, but she didn't have any better ideas.

"Want me to drive to his place?" Sally asked.

"No," Julia said. "You've still got your umbrella? You'll keep me safe enough."

Sally smiled. "And Rumpkin, of course," she said.

"That's right," Julia agreed. "Fierce, fierce Rumpkin."

Chapter 10

Most of the following day had been spent at the police station. Giving details of the night's attack had taken a surprising amount of time. And when they did finally get to talk to a constable, they had seemed wholly uninterested. Only name-dropping Mark's dad had managed to make her take the event vaguely seriously.

By the end of it, Julia was left feeling more bored than shaken but all the same she'd been glad when they had finally made it back late that afternoon.

Now, noises came from the bathroom. The shower running. Off-key singing. A hairdryer going full pelt. More off-key singing. From down in the living room, Julia listened to the sounds as they filtered down through the ceiling and did her best to ignore them and read her book.

Eventually, the sounds stopped and Sally emerged. She looked nothing short of glamorous. She wore dark, well-fitting jeans and one of her strappy red tops. Julia had to begrudgingly admit that the time spent on her hair had been worth it since her curls positively gleamed even in the dim light of the living room.

"Off to the shops?" Julia asked her, eyeing her over the top of her page.

Sally flashed a smile back at her. "I've got a date with Charlie. We're going to the Fox and Hounds."

Poor Sally. Living in Biddle Rhyne must be like being a bird in a cage, given its stunted offerings of nightlife.

"Have fun," Julia said.

"I will," Sally replied. "Don't wait up."

As it happened, Julia didn't need to.

About an hour and a half after Sally left, the front door banged open again and she came storming back in.

Julia sprang from her chair, book falling to the floor with a thud. She hadn't expected Sally back for hours, if at all, and she'd been on the verge of dozing off. The rude awakening left her in a flap. "What happened?" she asked.

Sally was red-faced and fuming. "He stood me up!" she said, flinging her handbag down violently on the sofa, sending a cushion falling onto Rumpkin and Rumpkin skittering to hide in the kitchen.

"Charlie didn't show up?" said Julia.

"No."

"Did he say why?"

"No. Nothing. He didn't answer my calls. He didn't reply to my texts. Nothing."

Julia thought for a moment as Sally stalked off into the kitchen and returned with a bottle of red, the cork already out. She had two glasses in hand so Julia supposed she had been volunteered into helping with this crisis.

"I wonder what happened to him," Julia murmured to herself as she accepted a glass.

"I don't care," Sally said. "Unless he's dead in a ditch somewhere I'm not forgiving him."

Julia couldn't help but worry that this might be a distinct possibility, but Sally was oblivious and started pulling old DVDs off the shelf and poking them with her toe in order to examine the titles.

"*10 Things I Hate About You*," Sally said at last, crouching down with a slight wobble and coming back up with the DVD.

Julia took a long sip of her wine. Sally was more put out than she had realized if she was going straight for the big guns. Sally's shift tomorrow was going to be fun; Julia only hoped that Charlie had sense enough to go straight home after work.

* * *

Julia watched anxiously, glancing back and forth between Sally and Charlie. Sally had been glaring daggers across the parlour the entire time since the work crew had come in after their shift.

Charlie for his part was making a concerted effort to be deep in conversation the whole time and therefore avoiding looking anywhere near the bar. He'd also been notably absent whenever it came time for someone to buy a round, nipping off towards the toilets or the smoking area.

"Look how red his eyes are, and the bags under them," Sally hissed to Julia. "You can tell he's been up all night. He must have been with someone else, the snake."

Julia said nothing but she had to agree, at least partially. He did look like someone who hadn't made it home the night before.

Before Julia could stop her, Sally had flipped the bar open with an echoing bang that brought her the attention of the whole pub and was striding across the room to Charlie's table.

"Well, isn't it nice of you to show up today?" Sally said, voice ringing across the narrow confines of the parlour.

Charlie couldn't meet her eye and looked down at his hands fidgeting with a bar mat on the table. "Yeah, I'm sorry about yesterday." He spoke quietly and Julia instinctively craned forward to hear. "Something came up."

"I bet it did," Sally snapped. "And what was her name?"

Charlie ignored the jeers that rose up from all around him. "No, no, it wasn't anything like that," he said.

"Well, what is it like, then?" Sally said.

Charlie looked silently at his hands for a moment, biting his lip. "I've been sworn to secrecy," he said eventually.

"Ha!" said Sally. "Pull the other one."

"No, it's true," Charlie said, pleadingly. "Look, can you just trust me? I'll make it up to you?"

Sally turned, her blonde ponytail flying out with an impressive flick as she did so, and began to march back towards the bar.

"I could buy you dinner?" Charlie called hopefully after her.

Sally didn't reply, but Julia saw just the slightest flickering of a smile on her lips as she shimmied her way back through the gap in the bar and carried on through the rear door and out of sight. Evidently she sensed that she'd drawn blood.

At Charlie's table, a hubbub of conversation rose up and one of the other builders got up and crossed the stone floor to the bar with deliberate casualness.

"Another pint?" Julia asked, her tone oozing sweetness as though she hadn't just witnessed the altercation between their friends.

"Yes, please, love," the man said, although Julia could see an almost full glass at the table where he'd been sitting.

Choosing to ignore that, she picked up an empty glass and began to pull.

"You know," the man started, hesitantly, suddenly finding the label on the beer pumps extremely engaging. "Charlie's not such a bad guy."

"Sally doesn't think so," Julia observed.

"I mean there won't be another girl. He's not like that," he said.

"No? Well, why did he stand her up then?" Julia said as the glass continued to fill.

The man gave a weary sigh and dropped his voice almost to a whisper. "He's just got money problems, that's all."

"Oh?" Julia prompted, leaning in in order to hear.

"Yeah. He went independent a couple of years back. Started his own business. Caught just the wrong time for furlough, though, and he lost everything. Not his fault, not in the slightest. But now he's got debts and all sorts. He takes any job that comes his way, and flogs himself something terrible trying to make ends meet.

"I wouldn't be surprised if he was moonlighting on some other site last night. Or just passed out tired after doing that for a few nights in a row. Of course, he can't say anything here because if the foreman overheard..." He nodded meaningfully at the table nearby where the foreman was still writing up his paperwork. "Well, it's against Charlie's contract, he'd be out on his ear. And he can't afford that."

Julia placed the beer in front of him, foam overflowing the top and sliding down the sides.

"Maybe you could have a word with your friend," the builder said as he held his card to the reader.

Julia nodded. "I'll let her know."

* * *

The fire wasn't lit, but that Saturday it was hotter than ever in the pub from the press of bodies crowded into the parlour.

Julia had never understood the appeal of football, but it must be an important match because Ivan had wheeled the TV into the parlour from out back and people had flocked in.

It was also important enough that Mark, usually so industrious, had taken the day off to go and watch the match at a pub in King's Barrow. He claimed he was at danger of losing his reserved spot if he didn't show up soon.

Not that Julia begrudged him the occasional day off after all the hard work he'd put in, she tried to convince herself as she pulled another pint and placed it down on the bar.

Her thoughts were disrupted by a horrible grinding noise that set Julia's teeth on edge. It seemed to be coming from behind the pub, but it was loud enough to be heard over the crowded chatter of the parlour. For a moment she thought that the building work had resumed, but then she realized there was no way the crew were turning up today.

Julia exchanged a look with Ivan, who was standing next to her, helping try and keep up with the stream of drinks orders.

"No idea," Ivan said, answering her unspoken question. "Go and check."

Julia finished pouring one last pint and then ducked back through the staff exit and down the corridor into the beer garden. She was greeted with the sight of a man's backside. The man attached to it was bent double, pushing something along the ground towards the car park, in a manner slightly reminiscent of a dung beetle.

The man grunted and pushed, and Julia realized what he was doing. He was rolling one of the plant pots along the patio, the spruce tree hanging limply still from the pot and leaving a trail of needles behind as it went. From the scratch marks etched deep in the patio, it looked like he'd tried dragging the pot before deciding to roll it, which would explain the awful noise Julia had heard from the pub.

"Just what do you think you're doing?" she said.

The man turned and straightened to his full, rather imposing height. It was Lance Teller. He was bright red in the face, and if his expression was anything to go by, it wasn't just from the exertion of moving the plant pot, he looked thoroughly cross.

"What does it look like I'm doing?" he growled. Julia resisted the urge to retreat a step back towards the safety of the pub. Lance jabbed a finger at the upturned pot. "I'm taking back my pots."

"Your pots?" said Julia.

"Yes, that's right, my pots," said Lance. He thumped his chest with his fist. "I made them. They're mine. That harlot had no right to sell them."

Julia opened her mouth to defend her friend, when Ivan came striding out of the pub and placed himself in front of her.

"Ivan," Julia began, "Lance said–"

"I heard," Ivan said, his tone matter of fact.

"They're my pots," Lance said again.

Ivan held his palms up. "Lance," he said. "You can take the pots. That's fine. There's no need to get angry."

"He can't take them, Ivan," Julia said. "We paid for those pots."

"I paid for them," Ivan reminded her. "And I don't mind if he takes them."

Lance put one foot up on the pot beside him and stood smirking at Julia.

Ivan laid a hand gently on Julia's shoulder. "Go on back inside. The queue will be manic. Let me handle this, all right?"

Julia hesitated for a moment, but she could see she wasn't going to win. Then another thought struck her: the inspector would be wanting a chat with Lance now he'd surfaced from wherever he'd been lurking.

"Fine," Julia said.

She gave one final look over her shoulder before going back in. Ivan and Lance were stood close together over the fallen pot, deep in conversation about something. She could only hope Ivan was convincing the other man to leave quietly.

Julia shut the door before they spotted her watching, then pulled her phone from her back pocket and found Jones's number. 'Lance Teller here at the Barley Mow right now', she messaged.

Just a couple of seconds later her phone chimed back in reply. It simply read, 'On my way'.

She stuffed the phone away again and took a few moments to compose herself, taking a few deep breaths before heading back into the parlour.

Ivan hadn't been wrong about the queue. In their short absence it seemed half the pub had finished their drinks and found it necessary to head up for a refill.

Julia quickly set to work, filling glasses as fast as she could. By the time she had served one or two customers, she was relieved to see Ivan appear back beside her and start pouring as well.

Julia realized that Jones's quarry would be long gone by the time he arrived. But maybe Ivan would know where he was going. She leaned sideways towards Ivan, keeping her voice low, at least relative to those on the other side of the bar. "I expect you sent Lance packing," she said.

"He's not gone anywhere," Ivan said. It was hard to read his expression; he looked flustered but whether that was from his encounter with Lance or the manic bar work or both was hard to tell. He gave a slight nod of his head to the far corner.

Julia's gaze followed where Ivan had indicated. Lance had joined the clutch of men sitting in the far corner by the unlit fire.

"You let him come in?" Julia hissed.

Ivan didn't answer her. He rang up the drink he was pouring, then stationed himself down at the other end of the short bar, and took an order there. Julia fumed as she poured the next drink. He'd have been well within his rights to turf Lance out for the way he had taken the plant pots, he certainly didn't need to have welcomed the man into his pub.

The conversation at Lance's table, already raucous, had amped up a level since he joined them and frequently some clatter of glasses or bellowing voice would cause Julia to look instinctively in their direction. Whenever she did so, Lance made sure to catch her eye from across the crowded room and she would quickly look back to whatever she was doing.

After what felt like an age of this game going on, the parlour door opened and the broad figure of DI Jones stood framed in the doorway.

Lance's group of friends gave a collective jeer but the rest of the pub, sensing the tension in the air, lapsed into a muttering quiet.

Jones crossed the small stretch of flagstones towards the group, Lance watching him approach with a half empty pint of beer in his hand and a mocking grin spread across his face.

Jones looped his thumbs into his belt and stood looking down at Lance, considering him. "Hello, Lance," he said eventually.

Lance sat back and hung an arm over the back of his seat. "Inspector," he said cheerfully.

Jones exhaled heavily through his nostrils. "Nice of you to grace us with your presence again. I need to establish your whereabouts last week," he said.

Lance gave a lazy shrug of his shoulders. "Sure. I've been with my dad the last few weeks. Down Trowbridge way."

"Right," Jones replied. "So if I went back to the station and called my colleagues in the Trowbridge constabulary then they'll be able to verify this?"

"Of course," Lance said, supplying the inspector with his dad's name.

Jones gave a curt nod and turned to go. As he did so, he caught Julia's eye behind the bar. She gave him a pleading look, not wanting to be left alone in the bar with Lance.

The policeman seemed to read her mind and altered his course, heading to the bar. The press of bodies parted as he approached.

"Julia, perhaps you'd be as good as to get me a coffee while I make a couple of calls."

While Julia turned and busied herself with the coffee machine, she could hear Jones talking in a low voice on his mobile.

She turned back just as Jones finished his call, placing his phone on the bar and taking up one of the suddenly vacant stools in the vicinity.

"Just waiting for someone to check something," he explained as Julia placed the steaming cup down next to his mobile.

Lance's voice piped up again, addressing his table but clearly audible across the bar. "Lads, did I ever tell you the story of my great-grandad, Frederick Teller?" he asked.

Julia squeezed her eyes shut. Lance took the opportunity to tell the story almost every time he was in, and without fail if the inspector was there, too. There was little wonder Jones was no longer a regular. She had hoped he would have had the good sense not to tell it tonight. It seemed she hoped for too much.

Lance took a long swig of his drink and soaked in his audience before continuing. "This was a long time ago, mind. Back when it was fairly common for people to bring drinks like fine French brandy in on the Cornish coast and smuggle them up the country, avoiding the excise on them.

"Now it so happened that my great-grandad lived in Trowbridge and he used to frequent a coaching inn there. Tremendous place it was. Warm and friendly and everything that a pub should be. Not unlike this place," he said, raising his glass towards the bar and meeting Julia's eyes once again.

Jones was sitting with his back to this, upright in his stool and unflinching. With controlled slowness he lifted the coffee to his lips and took a sip.

Lance continued. "And one night, as my old Frederick was enjoying a drink, a lad comes bursting in through the door, not more than eight or nine years old, and hollers at the top of his lungs that the excise man is coming, driving his horse something horrid.

"Now this poses a problem, of course, since Frederick was enjoying a finger or two of French brandy, as were most of the pub, and it might not have had excise paid on it in the strictest sense.

"So, quick as they can manage, and it might be that a few of them were a little worse for the brandy already, the men in the pub, my great-grandfather among them, haul the brandy barrel out of the door and into the village square.

"At this point they can already hear the hoofbeats coming in their direction, which means they've only got seconds, at most. And they look desperately for somewhere, anywhere to hide this blasted barrel before they're caught red-handed with it.

"'Into the duck pond!' my great-grandfather whispers, and the men haul the barrel into the pond with an almighty splash.

"But now there's another problem! No sooner have they dumped the barrel in there, than it bobs right back up into view. The blessed thing floats!

"So my great-grandad, he grabs a hay rake from next to the pond and he's desperately trying to push the thing under the water, but the best he can do is hold it down using the rake.

"And at this point our copper, the excise man, rides into view. And he looks down from his horse at my great-grandfather and he demands to know what he's doing in the middle of the night, poking his hay rake into the village duck pond.

"So my great-grandfather, he turns to the excise man, holding the brandy barrel down in the water the whole time, and he thickens his accent up and says 'Why, sir, isn't it obvious? I'm trying to get this here cheese out of the duck pond so I can have some supper!'

"And the excise man peers over into the duck pond and there looking back at him is the gert big reflection of the full moon overhead. And the copper laughs and says 'Oh, you foolish yokel. That's a reflection of the moon, you dolt.'

"With that the excise man jumps down and strides into the pub, looking for the brandy. And while he's inside they hoik the barrel out with the rake and roll it down the hill. Safe and sound for the next night."

Lance sat back, satisfied with his rendition and there was a smattering of laughter from around the table.

DI Jones still hadn't stirred and kept his gaze fixed on the row of spirits in front of him, but Julia could see his jaw clenching.

There was a sudden loud buzz that made Julia jump and the detective's phone lit up on the bar top. Jones snatched it up and listened, making a few brief interjections here and there before hanging up.

Lance crossed the room, propping one elbow lazily on the bar next to Jones, his face just a few inches away.

"Well, Detective?" Lance asked. "Did my dad vouch for me?"

"No need, was there, Lance?" Jones turned on his stool to face Lance, speaking slowly and picking his words with care. "Since you were in the nick in Trowbridge on the day in question."

A ripple of laughter went round the table and Lance's smile managed to spread even wider. "Oh, right, right. I'd forgotten about that, Detective. Awfully sorry, it just totally slipped my mind." He turned his attention to Julia. "Another pint, please, love."

Julia moved to pick up a glass but Jones raised his hand, causing her to stop.

"You've had more than enough," the detective said. "Evidently it's made your memory go all fuzzy. Best you were gone, I reckon. Go and sleep it off somewhere."

There was a pause while Lance considered his next move. He leaned one elbow on the bar and spoke to Jones in a low voice which Julia could only just catch over the background noise of the parlour. "Come on, Jonesy. One more, for old times' sake?"

Jones replied only by staring straight ahead, through the steam rising from his drink.

Lance glared for a few moments at the side of the older man's face before giving a theatrical sigh. "Perhaps you're right, Inspector," Lance said finally.

He aimed a wink in Julia's direction and then turned and called across the bar. "I think I'm off, lads. Take care now."

With all eyes in the pub on him, Lance swaggered across the flagstones to the door. He paused with one hand on the latch and turned to his drinking companions. "Say, lads. Do any of you have a rake I could borrow?"

Amidst the roar of barking laughter, Lance stepped out of the pub and the door clicked shut behind him.

Jones put his hand on his mug but didn't lift it, Julia could see his knuckles whitening around it. She couldn't help wondering what 'old times' Lance had been referring to, but Jones still had his distant stare, looking straight through Julia, and she couldn't help but think this was the wrong time to ask.

She laid one hand lightly on top of Jones's. "Thank you, Rhys," she said quietly.

Jones didn't reply, except to make a huffing sound through his nose, but she felt his hand untense and he picked the coffee cup up and drained it.

He placed the cup back down onto its saucer and seemed to peer into its depths for a minute. "I'll be off," he said, seemingly to the world in general, and slid down from the stool.

Chapter 11

Things in the pub began to settle down after Lance and the inspector had left. The match started and then, as Julia had predicted it would, finished. The football crowd thinned out a bit and then a lot.

The sun dipped down below the horizon and Ivan stacked up the logs in the fire and soon had a crackling blaze going; the atmosphere, if not the cosy sitting-room feel that the parlour normally had, at least had lost the edge of earlier in the day.

There was a lull in the drinks orders, the first in some hours, and Julia took the opportunity to slip through into the cool and quiet of the staff corridor, leaving the door open so she could keep an eye on the parlour.

She leaned back against the whitewashed wall, stretching out her aching back, and allowed herself a long sigh, puffing her cheeks out.

"Tough day, huh?"

The words made Julia jump, she hadn't realized that Ivan had emerged from the cellar, presumably changing a barrel down there.

For most of the afternoon the two of them had stood side by side in icy silence as they poured drinks for the crowded bar.

Julia was still bristling with how Ivan had let Lance steal back the plant pots, not to mention stood by while he riled up the inspector. But he seemed in a conciliatory mood now, and she didn't have the energy to fight. She gave a little nod.

Ivan let out a sigh of his own, placing one hand on the top of the door frame and leaning there, looking out over his pub and the handful of tables still occupied.

"It's not easy for me just to tell him to naff off, as tempting as that would be," Ivan said, reading the thoughts going through Julia's head. "Lance and me, we go way back. He's been a regular here for a long time – sometimes when the pub wasn't in such great shape, in the way of customers. Actually, Lance and Rhys used to be good mates, once upon a time."

That was news to Julia. "Really?" she asked, her interest piqued.

The landlord nodded. "Not that they were super close or anything. But they were both regulars here, as you know. Used to do the quiz together. Which worked well for everyone else since they rarely got two questions right between them." He gave a rueful chuckle to himself.

That explained what Lance had meant by 'old times' sake' then, Julia thought. "What happened, then?" she asked.

"Oh, you know," Ivan said, straightening back up. "Rhys was rising through the ranks of the police force. Lance was, shall we say, going in the opposite direction. The friction became a bit too much so Jones bowed out and stopped coming. It's not so easy keeping friends when you're a copper, I suppose."

Julia had to agree. The inspector was a nice enough man, when you didn't meet him in a professional capacity.

But she had noted that his social circle was little more than a dot.

"Ah, it's been a strange few days, Julia," Ivan said, still reminiscing. "Seeing all these old faces again. Lance. Rhys. And Graham the other day as well. He used to be one of my regulars, too. Back in the day. It's just a shame not to see them under better circumstances. I'm sure everything used to be a lot simpler around here."

Julia was a bit surprised that Jones had brought Graham into the Barley Mow after intercepting him in the fields the other day. She knew that the inspector defaulted to 'a stiff drink' as a way of recovering from a shock, but it hardly seemed appropriate for Mr West. After the shock of his daughter's remains being found and then stolen, something more tactful would have been better. Not to mention the fact that the pub would have been filled with the gawkers and lookie-loos who had flocked in to see what the police presence was all about. Surely Mr West didn't need to be subjected to that?

Julia tutted angrily as she mulled Jones's behaviour. Ivan should really have known better than to serve him under the circumstances, too. But the landlord would undoubtedly prescribe a drink for any ailment, big or small, and it would probably be pointless to start another row with her boss.

Through the doorway, Julia spotted a customer heading up to the bar and she pointed towards him. "I'd better go," she said to Ivan.

Ivan blinked, coming back from wherever his mind had been. "Nah, you go on and get home," he said to Julia. "I can cope on my own here and you've had a long day."

Julia accepted the peace offering and summoned up the energy to smile. "Thanks, Ivan," she said, and as Ivan headed back to the pumps she made for the kitchen exit and then slipped out into the darkness.

It was only late afternoon but the sun had already set some time ago. Across the car park, she could see Sally waiting for her, standing next to Ivan's ridiculous haystack. Unsurprisingly, Ivan's marketing hadn't really made the pub any busier than it already had been – football notwithstanding.

Sally was idly teasing loose strands of hay from one of the bales as she approached.

"Are you okay, Sally?" Julia asked. "Ready to go?"

"Hm," Sally hummed in reply. "Do you think Ivan realized that he could have built this thing much taller if he hadn't made it so wide?" she asked.

The thought had struck Julia before that it wasn't the most sensible way to build a giant haystack. If that wasn't a contradiction in terms. It would have had more impact if it was higher. "It's strange, isn't it?" Julia said.

Sally placed two hands on the hay and put her head right against it, her eye against the join between two of the bales. "It isn't just strange, it's hollow," she said.

Julia stepped closer to the haystack and put her own eye to one of the cracks. Sally was right, the haystack was built as a big, hollow square. Although what, if anything, was inside the thing was impossible to tell in this light.

"I wonder what's in there," Julia muttered, straining against the darkness to no avail.

"I don't know," Sally said. She gave one of the bales an experimental tug and managed to shift it slightly. "But I want to find out. If Ivan's secretly building another house or swing set or something then I want to know about it before I'm named on the inevitable lawsuit that it causes."

Further down the car park a car door slammed. A group of women were making their way towards the pub, talking and laughing as they went. "Maybe not now, though, Sally. Ivan would get wind of us in no time," said Julia.

"Fine, but I still want to know what he's up to in there," Sally said and shoved the hay bale back into place with a grunt.

Chapter 12

The knife slashed, cutting easily through the brown tape, and the lid of the cardboard box popped open.

Inside were books. Dozens of lovely new books. Julia delved her hands into the box and began hauling them out.

With the painting finished over the weekend and the shelves in place, Mark was finally liberated to go and perform paid work. But before doing so, he had dropped off a vanload of cardboard boxes filled with books. Boxes which had been filling his parents' garage for the previous week. Julia had spent a happy afternoon putting them onto their shelves.

Their strategy meant putting the local-interest books and true crime in pride of place by the window, hoping to make full use of the brief local-media flurry Julia had caused when she solved Mrs White's murder. These were the books which she unpacked first, proudly displaying them to the high street as if to say to the world 'yes, we really are going to be a bookshop soon'.

She finished filling the units by the window and stood back to admire her handiwork. A few copies of a book describing the unlikely criminal underbelly of a small northern village hadn't fitted on and remained in the box. Still, Julia supposed, it was good to have some stock in the back.

As she stood watching, she saw Ivan's head bobbing along outside the window, travelling up the high street.

It wasn't entirely unknown for the landlord to leave the boundaries of the Barley Mow, but there was always something there that needed doing and it was unusual enough to strike Julia. She realized a moment later that he'd be on his way to the parish council meeting, where they'd be deciding the fate of his house building endeavours on the site of the old coach house. He was attending then, despite all of his earlier bluster.

Curiosity got the better of her and Julia quickly shoved the remaining books back into their box and grabbed her coat, making for the door.

She locked the front door of the bookshop and hurried down the broad stone steps to the high street. Ivan was now only a dark figure under one of the street lights further up the road. But that was fine, Julia wasn't sure what temper he'd be in before the meeting and wasn't overly keen to find out, so she trailed along behind at a safe distance.

There were more people than she expected when they reached the school. The brightly lit assembly hall had a couple of dozen or so in attendance, forming small groups on the uncomfortable little plastic chairs that had been set out facing the stage, so she easily managed to slip into a chair near the back unnoticed while Ivan took his reserved seat in the front row.

The school hall itself was a plain, utilitarian building, lined on two sides with large windows that stretched from hip height up to the low roof, looking out on the tarmac playground, dark and empty this late in the day. The school had tried their best to liven the room up with colourful and supposedly inspirational paintings on the other two walls, many done by the pupils and showcasing an endearing lack of talent.

Despite the clock over the stage hitting six, nothing appeared to be happening in the way of proceedings and the members of the audience continued to talk amongst themselves in low voices.

Around quarter past the hour, Ivan rose from his seat at the front of the room and in one large movement stepped up onto the low stage. He loomed over the row of councillors, who were sitting in a line at the table set up there. They were too far away for Julia to hear what was being said but no one seemed to be very happy.

Eventually there was a general nodding and shrugging from the councillors and Ivan stepped back off the stage and settled into his chair again with his arms folded. The councillor seated in the middle of the row stood up and gradually the conversations in the audience fell quiet.

"Ladies and gentlemen," the councillor said, raising their voice to be heard over the one or two people in the audience who hadn't noticed the hush. "I'm afraid that due to the unexpected absence of the council's representative from the planning department, Mr Peabody, this extraordinary session of Biddle Parish Council is cancelled, with the aim of rescheduling on the next convenient date. Apologies and thank you all for your continued input into your local community."

"And the temporary suspension order?" Ivan prompted from the audience.

The councillor looked at him. "Yes, right. The temporary suspension order is suspended. Er, temporarily. You may continue work for the time being."

With that the councillor took up a small wooden gavel and banged it smartly on the table, which seemed rather final. There was a ripple of murmured surprise among the gathered residents as they rose and broke up into small knots and made towards the exit.

Julia did her best to keep her head down and remain unobtrusive as she went along near the back of the stream of people, but she heard her name being called across the school hall and turned to see Ivan striding towards her.

"Great to see you here, Julia," Ivan boomed as his long legs quickly closed the distance. "Come to show your support, have you?"

"Yes, exactly," Julia said, not meeting her boss's eye. As long as he didn't ask which side she was supporting, then what he said was broadly true, she supposed.

"I'm sorry your meeting didn't go ahead," she added.

"Sorry?" Ivan said. "Why are you sorry?"

"I'm sure you wanted to get everything sorted sooner rather than later," Julia said.

Ivan smiled down at her as they passed out into the school grounds. "No, this is a good thing. That runt from the planning department obviously had it in for me. The more work I can get done before the ruling, the better it will go for me. If I've got proper foundations and pipework in, they're far more likely to see the potential of what I'm doing and tell me to crack on."

Julia nodded thoughtfully although she still wasn't convinced by Ivan's logic. He always seemed to run far more on self-interest and bloody-mindedness than any real consideration of facts or reasoning. But it had got him this far in the world so Julia supposed that she shouldn't be too quick to dismiss it.

She walked along the side of the road in silence as Ivan continued to expound the wonders of the houses he was building. She wondered if this was a speech he had rehearsed for the meeting that now had an audience of one, but it sounded pretty much off the cuff.

Just on the other side of the bookshop, she drew to a halt at a zebra crossing. "This is me," she said, indicating the narrow street on the other side.

Ivan gave her a wave. "Well, see you tomorrow, Julia. Time to go back and see what calamities have occurred at the pub in my absence."

"Goodnight, Ivan," Julia replied, hurrying across the road and down the side street.

The street was squeezed into a gap between two of the grander Victorian buildings on the high street. The sides of them were bare brick, devoid of any windows, and Julia kept up her quick pace, anxious to get through the dark tunnel the houses created.

Just as she was emerging from their shadows into the brighter street beyond, something glinting in the streetlight caught her eye. She crouched down to examine it.

"Oh, gosh," she murmured to herself, quickly glancing about to see if anyone was around, but she found herself alone.

She picked the item up and turned it round in her hands, examining it.

It was a cracked pair of spectacles. Innocuous enough in and of themselves. But she recognized the distinctive round frames as Mr Peabody's. It seemed he'd made it this close to the planning meeting before something – or someone – knocked the glasses from his face. Julia squinted at the specs as best she could in the dim light of the street. She couldn't be certain but there seemed to be a small, dark stain on the nosepiece. It looked like blood.

She looked round over her shoulder once more. Briefly, she saw a figure standing at the entrance of the alleyway, silhouetted by the lights of a passing car, watching her impassively. But when the next car went by a moment later they had gone.

Julia stood and hurried in the direction of home.

* * *

Julia was practically at a run by the time she arrived at the front door. She hadn't seen the shadowy figure again but every time she dared to look back she was convinced that she would see them there.

Fumbling with nerves, she rattled the key in the lock several times before finally getting it to turn and she stumbled into the house, smartly closing the door behind her and drawing the chain across after.

Sally emerged from the kitchen, apron on, and greeted her cheerfully. There was no smudge of flour across her cheek this time, since there was no audience.

"I've got a cake in the oven," Sally said, wiping her hands on her front.

Julia rushed quickly up to her friend. "Sally, what do you make of these?" she asked. She thrust the pair of spectacles she'd found towards her.

Sally took them gingerly and held them up to the light. "They're broken," she observed, accurately.

"What about that?" Julia said, pointing to the nosepiece. "Does that look like blood to you?"

Sally held the glasses closer and squinted at them. "Hard to tell," she murmured. "It could be anything really. Blood, a bit of mud. I'm not sure."

Julia quickly relayed all about the planning meeting and Mr Peabody being unexpectedly missing. "Do you think we should call the police?" Julia asked when she finished.

Sally looked thoughtful. "Do you need to wait forty-eight hours? Or is that just something in the films?"

"I'll call Mark's dad at least," Julia said.

She pulled her phone out of her handbag and thumbed through the address book. She was just about to hit the call button when Sally gave a startled little cry.

"Oh, no!" Sally gasped, her face suddenly going pale.

"What?" Jullia hissed.

"It's burning!" Sally cried, and turned and dashed into the kitchen.

Julia scowled after her and called Jones.

* * *

Julia sat in the armchair, Rumpkin drawn in near to her. Despite his initial protests, the dog had settled down and was now sound asleep.

The room had lapsed into silence as they waited for Jones to arrive, broken only by Rumpkin's intermittent, rattling snores. Julia twisted a stray strand of his hair, listlessly.

She sat forward. "I've been thinking," she said.

Sally was nestled into the cushions on the sofa next to Julia. "About?" she prompted.

"About who might have hurt Mr Peabody."

Sally struggled up into a sitting position. "Who?" she asked.

Julia took in a deep breath, wondering if she should voice her suspicions aloud. She would have to tell the inspector when he arrived at any rate, she might as well tell Sally now. "I think it could have been Ivan," she said.

"Ivan? No, he wouldn't be capable of something like that, would he?" Sally said, but Julia could hear the doubt creeping in at the edge of her voice.

Julia gave a shrug, or as much as one as she could manage around Rumpkin. "I don't know. I mean, he's always had a temper, hasn't he? And he was convinced that delaying this council meeting was good for the houses he's trying to build."

"Yes, I know he's got a temper," Sally replied, "but I don't think he's ever been violent to anyone."

They sat quietly, the house silent except for the sound of the smoke alarm going off in the kitchen.

Julia's eyes widened. "You don't think Ivan might have been the one to hurt Barry as well, do you?"

"No. What reason would he have to do that?" Sally asked.

"Barry would have seen that building work on the day it first started. Ivan told me that the longer the work is underway before the council finds out about it, the more chance they have of letting it continue. Maybe Barry said that he was going to tell the council about it and Ivan decided to stop him."

"So he turned up at his flat?" Sally said. She didn't seem convinced.

"Barry would have let Ivan in; Rhys said the killer was probably someone Barry knew."

"Perhaps," Sally said thoughtfully. "That building site wasn't going to stay a secret from the council for very long, though. You can't hide four houses going up in a pub beer garden. Even Biddle Parish Council would be on the ball to that. What would Ivan have gained? A few days of work before someone let the council know. It's not much to kill someone over."

Julia sighed. "Perhaps you're right. I hope you're right."

"Still," Sally said. "Maybe we should be a bit careful around Ivan, just in case."

As she said it, there was a pounding on the front door and Julia sprang up, depositing Rumpkin onto the carpet. She headed quickly across the room with Sally following not far behind.

Julia slid the door open on the chain and peered through the crack. She could see a sliver of DI Jones, a flinty expression on his face.

"Hang on, Rhys, I'll just open up," Julia said, closing the door again so she could slide the chain off and open it fully.

Jones stood filling the doorway "Julia. Sally," he said tersely. "May I come in?"

Julia stepped aside and let the inspector brush past her and into the living room. She shut the door on the cold night and hurried after him.

"Is there any news?" she asked, fidgeting with her hands. "Have they found him?"

"Nothing yet, but I've got a couple of uniforms out looking for him," Jones replied.

When he turned around he had his notebook open. "Now, let's go through what you told me one more time. He was meant to attend the planning meeting this evening but he didn't show up. On your way home you found his glasses, broken, on one of the side streets."

"That's right," Julia said.

Jones was scrawling notes at a rapid pace. "Which means he must live somewhere near you, I suppose. Now, I know he wasn't the most popular man. His job meant he ruffled quite a few feathers locally. Is that fair to say?"

Julia froze. The inspector finished writing and looked at her over the top of his notebook, pen still hovering over the page. "Julia?"

"I didn't kill him!" Julia squeaked. "I know we argued with him about the shop, but I didn't kill him, you have to believe me."

Jones breathed out heavily through his nose, face crumpling into a frown. "For pity's sake, Julia. I'm not accusing you of murder."

"Not accusing her of murder again, you mean," Sally put in, returning to the sofa.

The inspector's scowl deepened. "Yes. I mean I'm not accusing her of murder again. That was very much a one-time thing. I hope. And for the record, I didn't know you had argued with him about the shop."

Julia felt herself blushing but she was saved from replying as there was a smart knock at the door.

"You should get that," Jones said.

Julia couldn't meet his eye as she slipped past him and pulled open the front door.

A uniformed police constable stood there, and next to him, alive and well was Mr Peabody, wearing a pair of thick-lensed glasses with square frames.

"Oh, Mr Peabody," Julia exclaimed. "I'm so glad to see you." She stopped short of adding 'alive'.

Mr Peabody tapped the unwieldy looking glasses that sat on his nose. "Nice to see you as well," he said.

The policeman spoke, looking over Julia's head towards the inspector. "Sorry for just turning up, sir," he said, "but we were only just round the corner so I thought we might as well. Seems your phone was out of signal again."

"That ruddy phone," the inspector sighed. "Yes, thank you, Constable. That's quite all right. He was at home, was he?"

"At home and unharmed," the policeman replied.

"What happened then?" Sally asked, appearing at Julia's shoulder. "Why didn't you make the meeting?"

Mr Peabody cleared his throat. "Well, I was just on my way there when that dratted cat that Mrs Singh keeps leaped out of the shadows at me. I didn't see the thing until I almost trod on it. It scared the living daylights out of me, to tell you the truth."

The planning inspector looked slightly embarrassed as he carried on. "I think I must have dislodged my own glasses as I was flailing at it. I hurried back home to find my spare pair before the meeting but, well, I really can't find my glasses without my glasses. In fact, I really didn't manage much at all until my husband got home and rescued me. The police arrived shortly after. It would seem it's all caused quite a hoo-haa." He sighed. "That side street really is a hazard, it's so badly lit. Someone should do something about it, but it's not my department."

Julia gave a lopsided smile. "I'm glad you're okay, anyway. I was worried about you."

"Thanks for your concern," he said. "Other than missing the meeting, though, I think there's no harm done. There's always next month to hold the meeting. And the temporary suspension on the work will hold until then."

Julia thought about the temporary suspension's temporary suspension but decided to keep quiet. She'd let Ivan have this one. After accusing him of murder, even only to Sally, she rather felt she owed it to him.

Jones clapped his hands together. "I guess that about wraps that up, then," he said. "Shall we all get out of these ladies' hair?"

"Actually, while I'm here, Miss Ford," Mr Peabody said.

All eyes turned to the planning inspector.

"I've finished reviewing the proposed bookshop on the ex-library premises on Biddle High Street," he said.

Julia's heart sank. "Yes?"

"Everything appears to be in order," Mr Peabody said.

Julia managed to refrain from cheering. "Excellent," she said. "Thank you."

"Although, I'm missing documentation on the number and location of the fire exits. I've brought the forms here." He produced some crisply folded sheets of A4 from his coat and extended them towards Julia. "If you could try and get them to me at my office as soon as you can."

Julia did her best to smile and accepted the forms. She was still glad to see him alive and well. But ever so slightly less than she had been two minutes earlier.

"Tomorrow morning would be desirable," Mr Peabody said, before departing from her house.

No sooner had the front door closed behind him than the doorbell rang again, the gentle chimes filling the living room.

Julia shot Sally a questioning look.

"That will be Charlie," Sally said, as she trotted across the room towards the door.

"You're going out again?" Julia asked.

"Staying in," Sally called over her shoulder. "I didn't want to risk getting stood up a second time."

Well, that explained the baking, Julia thought to herself. Charlie wouldn't be the first man to become ensnared by her friend's superior skills in the kitchen.

Sally opened the door and there Charlie stood, wearing a smile and holding a cheap four-pack of cider in a cardboard wrapper.

Sally glanced down at the drinks offering as she stepped aside to let Charlie in. "Wow, only the finest for me, is it?" she said.

Charlie joined her looking at the cider cans. "What makes you think they're for you?" he asked.

Sally pouted. "I don't think I want you drinking all those. You still look tired, you'll be falling asleep on the sofa."

Charlie laughed. "I'll put these in the fridge, shall I?"

Julia hurried over and whispered in Sally's ear while her date was busy in the kitchen. "You should have said he was coming," she said. "I could have cleared out, you know."

"Oh, don't be silly," Sally replied. "I didn't want to turf you out, especially with all that business with Mr Peabody getting you worked up. You don't mind, do you?"

"No, it's fine," Julia said. "In fact, it will be nice knowing I'm not alone in the house."

Charlie came back into the living room, a single can of cider in his hand, already opened. Not that she touched the stuff, but Julia couldn't help thinking that the offer would have been nice and she decided to turn the screw before she got banished upstairs.

"Well, it's great that you could turn down the draw of moonlighting to see Sally," Julia said.

She saw just the faintest of twitches in Charlie's eye, and she was sure it was more than just his lack of sleep. "Or was the moonlighting not on offer?" she added.

"No, it was…" Charlie said, but there was something in his voice that made Julia sure he was holding back.

Sally must have picked up on it, too. "But?" she prompted.

Charlie looked deflated. "I really didn't fancy working with the new guy Ivan brought in," he mumbled.

"Ivan?" said Julia.

"New guy?" said Sally.

Charlie's shoulders slumped even further. "Yeah, I've been helping Ivan put in the septic tanks for his new houses in that daft hay stack of his."

"Ha!" Sally burst out, making Charlie jump. "I knew it."

"So, who is this new guy?" Julia asked.

"And why is he so objectionable?" Sally added.

Charlie took a long pull on his cider then licked his lips. "Do you know Lance Teller?"

"You could say that," Julia muttered darkly.

"Well, yeah, him," said Charlie.

"And why don't you want to work with him?" asked Sally "Just because he's a giant oaf?"

"Look, I shouldn't be telling you this," Charlie said. "It's all just rumours. But Aimiee West was in my year at school. When she disappeared, everyone reckoned Lance was the one who did it."

"What? Why?" Julia asked.

"He was always hanging around the girls in our year. Everyone thought he was creepy. Aimiee got most of his attentions. Until she went missing. Then he turned to Janice."

"Did you tell the police this?" said Julia.

Charlie gave a shrug. "I didn't. I'm not sure if anyone else did. But it wouldn't have mattered."

"Why not?"

"The cop looking for Aimiee. He was one of Lance's mates. So we all knew he wasn't going to do him for it."

Julia suddenly went cold. That cop would have been Jones.

Charlie shuffled awkwardly on the carpet. "Anyway, you can see why I didn't want to work with Lance, even if the money was good. Especially with Aimiee's bones suddenly turning up and everything."

Julia gasped.

"What did I say?" Charlie asked.

"Those bones didn't just turn up, but someone stole them," Julia said, before she could stop herself.

"Right, they scooped them up with the digger and dumped them in the rhyne," Charlie said.

"I probably shouldn't have said," Julia replied, regretting her sudden outburst. "The police wanted to keep it quiet. But someone went and took them from there before the police arrived."

Charlie swore quietly under his breath.

"But why would someone do something like that?" Sally said in a quiet voice.

"Maybe there's something about those bones that gives a clue to Aimiee's killer," Julia said. "Presumably whoever took them wanted to hide them somewhere no one would find them."

"Somewhere like underneath a septic tank," Charlie said.

The two women fell silent while this sank in.

"We should call the police," Charlie said.

Sally shook her head adamantly. "The police is still the same detective who's friends with Lance," she said.

"You can't think Jones would let Lance get away with that," Julia said.

"No, but if it does turn out to have been Lance and Jones let him slip by under his nose? That's got to be the end of his career, right? He's got every incentive not to investigate. That's just human nature."

"We should go up there," Julia said.

"What?" Sally blinked at her.

"Just to see what's going on," said Julia. "We know Lance will be putting the tanks down. We need to know nothing's going on there. Before Aimiee ends up under six feet of dirt."

Sally thought, but only for a moment. "Fine," she said. She turned to Charlie. "Sorry, looks like I'm standing you up this time."

"I'll come, too," Charlie said.

Sally was already reaching for her coat. "I can't ask you to do that," she said.

"But I can hardly let you two go off alone," Charlie said. "What if you get hurt?"

As much as Julia might have liked to have someone like Charlie around in case Lance did spot them, she still wasn't entirely sure how far she could trust him.

"Don't worry," she said. "We can take care of ourselves."

She really hoped that was true.

Chapter 13

Wrapped up well against the cold, Julia and Sally made their way down the side streets, heading for the Barley Mow. At this hour, everyone in the village was in bed and there was no traffic passing through on the high street. Everything seemed still and quiet; the only sound was the occasional call of an owl floating in from over the fields.

Julia and Sally reached the cut-through, a narrow alley between two gardens that led out onto the lane.

"We should turn these off, we don't want Lance to see us coming," Sally said, clicking off the torch on her phone and shoving it into her coat.

Julia turned her own off, ducked under the brambles overhanging from one of the gardens, and the two women emerged out onto the country lane.

It was almost pitch-black with their torches off. A few stars shone overhead but there was no moon. Not for the first time, Julia reflected that this might be a blooming stupid thing to do. The only saving grace was that they would hear the sound of a car for miles in either direction and could get out of the way.

They carried on along the lane in silence, no sign of any car or anyone else out that night. They rounded the bend in the road, knowing that the Barley Mow was ahead of them now but it was only visible as a dark outline against the patchwork of stars.

Without warning, Sally stopped in her tracks, grabbing Julia by the arm with both hands. "There," she hissed, her voice just a whisper in the darkness. "Do you see?"

"Yes," Julia replied, equally quiet.

A little white light bobbed and weaved alongside the unlit building. The pub had only closed ten or fifteen minutes ago, but it seemed that Lance was already at work.

"We'd better hurry," Julia said, starting along the lane again as quickly as she dared in the blackness.

As they neared the pub, a high-pitched whistle carried over to them on the breeze, although it was no tune that Julia recognized. She slowed down as she felt gravel shift noisily under her foot.

Julia glanced over at her friend, barely visible in the darkness despite being only inches away. Sally gave a tiny nod of her head and they carried on across the car park of the pub. They were really doing this then.

They crept on, the dark silhouette of the haystack growing larger and the dancing light growing brighter. They trod gently over the gravel but the tiniest noise of shifting stones sounded like an avalanche in the stillness of the night.

When they were about halfway across the car park, the whistling stopped. Julia and Sally froze midstride, wondering if they'd been overhead. The torchlight swung out across them and Julia's heart froze. But the beam carried on its arc and then disappeared inside the haystack. After standing stock-still for a moment or so, they continued their stealthy approach. The torch was just visible as a line of light between the bales.

Reaching the haystack, the two women began to climb. Julia went first, hands grasping on the bales, the hay surprisingly sharp even through her gloves.

Amazingly, Julia reflected as she realized what a perfectly stupid idea this was, this had been part of the plan she and Sally had put together. They'd noticed a larger gap in the bales about halfway up where they hadn't been stacked neatly together. This, they reckoned, would be a good place to peek inside.

In the gentle light of their living room with the gas fire purring away, it had sounded like a good idea.

Now, in the freezing cold, halfway up the wall of hay with Sally clambering after her, Julia only wished they were back there, Rumpkin snoring happily on her lap.

But they had come this far. Julia's groping hand reached the gap in the bales and she lifted herself up. The gap here was almost the size of one of the bales themselves, and with a bit of shuffling and wriggling, she managed to wedge herself into the hole on all fours.

There was a quiet rustling as Sally appeared next to her, puffing slightly with the exertion of her climb.

Julia peered down into the interior of the haystack, at first unable to believe what she was seeing.

The inside was indeed hollow as they had guessed. In the far wall, the one facing the pub, several of the bales had been removed to form a doorway. That must have been done that night, as it definitely hadn't been there before.

A large square of the ground inside had been cleared. The gravel had been scraped away to form a bank against one of the walls of the haystack and it looked like there was a deep hole dug in the middle.

And getting deeper. Lance was busy at work inside, a shovel rising and falling, depositing earth onto a growing pile at one side of the hole. He was working by the light of a bright, white torch affixed to the hard hat he wore.

"At least we got here while he's still digging," Julia whispered. "He can't have put anything in that hole yet."

There was a shuffling sound from beside her, which Julia gathered was Sally nodding.

"What do we do now?" Sally asked.

"I guess we just wait," Julia said. "We can't do anything until he brings those bones out from wherever he's hidden them. Otherwise he can just deny everything."

"And then we pounce?" said Sally.

"And then we call Jones," Julia replied firmly.

"Even though he might have covered for Lance?"

"He won't cover for *that*," Julia said. "Even an old friend couldn't talk their way out of it if they've actually got the bones on them."

Sally hummed in reply, she didn't sound convinced.

The night went on and grew colder. Even huddled up next to each other between the hay bales, the chill set in deeply.

All the time Lance worked, whistling on and off as he did so. But the hole just kept getting deeper. For hours he dug, taking the earth away in a wheelbarrow every so often. He never seemed to put anything into the hole.

If it weren't for the discomfort of being jammed into their little nook, Julia might have started to doze off. But suddenly her ears pricked up. Footsteps crunched on the gravel.

"Someone's coming," Julia whispered.

"Who?"

"How should I know?"

Apparently Lance had the same question because he clambered from his hole to stick his head through the makeshift door, the shovel still clutched tightly in his hands. "Who's there?" he asked, his voice incredibly loud after the stillness of the night.

"It's me," a voice came in reply. "Charlie."

"Charlie?" Lance said. "What are you doing here?"

There was a slight pause before the reply. "I decided I needed that extra cash after all."

Lance gave a loud sigh. "Well, you took long enough to decide, didn't you? I'm almost done here."

"You've put the tanks in?" Charlie asked.

Lance gave a sharp laugh. "Not even started. Your hole was nowhere near deep enough. The tanks will be tomorrow night's job now."

"Oh."

Lance leaned his shovel up against the nearest bale. "Tell you what, finish loading up one last barrow and tidy up for the night and I'll cut you in for a tenner."

"Fine," Charlie replied.

With that, Lance sauntered out through the hole and another figure appeared. There was a brief fumbling and Charlie's torch sprang to life, casting strange shadows about the inside of the hay stack as he swung it all around, but failed to spot Julia and Sally's perch.

"You can come out," Charlie said quietly. "He's gone."

Julia shuffled awkwardly forwards and managed to find a foothold to lower herself down, dropping the last foot or so to land on the soil.

"What are you doing here?" Julia asked, still keeping her voice low, as Sally clambered down next to her.

"I was worried," Charlie said. "You'd been gone for hours."

Julia rubbed her frozen hands together, trying to get some warmth into them. "All you missed was a load of digging," Julia said.

It was hard to tell with the torch shining at her, but Julia thought Charlie was looking a little sheepish.

"I'm sure those holes were deep enough for the tanks," Charlie said.

"We'll just have to come back again tomorrow night," Julia said.

"Come on," Sally said to Julia. "Let's get back home, I'm freezing."

"I'll walk you back," Charlie said.

"Don't you have work to do?" Sally said.

"But—"

"I did say we could look after ourselves, didn't I?" said Sally.

She strode off towards the door in the hay bales. After two steps, she slipped as the uneven ground beneath her shifted and she flung an arm out to catch her balance.

Pretending this didn't happen, she carried on out into the night.

* * *

125

Julia was laying the tables in the dining room ahead of the pub opening its doors, but she was fighting to keep her eyes open. Even when she'd finally gotten to bed she couldn't sleep, constantly playing through in her mind what Lance might be up to.

And it still bothered her that Ivan would allow Lance to drink in the pub, let alone work for him. Surely he would have known the rumours from when Aimiee disappeared?

A thought struck Julia and she froze with cutlery in her hands. What if Ivan did know what was underneath those swings the whole time? Julia had only been young but she seemed to remember that they went up rather suddenly.

But would he have risked digging them up? Even with the lure of selling the land for homes?

Maybe Ivan had Lance ready to swoop in and take the bones away? He'd been the one to call the builders in for lunch. If she and Sally hadn't been out there on their break – against Ivan's orders – no one would have seen the digger taking them. At least not until they'd made a clean getaway. No one would have known the bones were there.

Subconsciously, Julia drifted to the window that looked out over the hay bales, wondering what might happen there that night.

"What are you doing there?"

Julia jumped half out of her skin and turned to find Ivan right beside her.

He looked down at her with a dark scowl.

With a deliberate slowness, he reached out and plucked his apron up from the back of one of the chairs.

"Those tables won't lay themselves," he said, tying the apron up as he headed off again. He muttered to himself as he went. "And the barrels won't change themselves, either."

Alone in the room again, Julia felt her heart pounding. Was she being unfair to Ivan? In all the years she'd known him, he'd never harmed a fly.

All the same she couldn't help feeling the urge to sneak after him and lock him down in the cellar until she knew for sure what was going on.

Instead, she stole another glance round at the hay stack and let out a small shriek as she found a face nose-to-nose with her through the window.

Jones held his hands up apologetically. "Sorry, I didn't mean to scare you," he said, his raised voice just audible through the thin glass. "I was just trying to see if you were there."

Julia let out a deep breath and indicated for him to go around to the parlour and she went round to unlock the door.

"What are you doing here, Rhys?" she said.

The inspector looked distinctly uncomfortable, and remained standing just outside the door.

"I was passing by this way," Jones said. "But there was something that I wanted to tell you."

"Oh?"

Jones tugged at the side of his moustache before replying. "They found Aimiee's bones last night. Well, we'll have to wait for the lab to confirm but I think we can be fairly certain. I wanted you to hear it from me rather than through the papers or one of the local gossips."

Julia blinked. She was suddenly much more awake. "Found them where?" she asked.

"One of the constables spotted them about a mile up the road," Jones replied, flapping an arm in the general direction. "He got called out to a break-in at a farm a bit before midnight. Turned out to be a wild goose chase. Almost literally. But on his drive back, he saw them. A shallow grave just off the road."

"No, that's awful," Julia muttered.

"Well, it was a funny business," Jones said. "Whoever buried her marked the grave with a wooden cross. It seemed they wanted them to be found. And seems they'd treated the remains with some respect, going through that effort."

"Hmm, not Lance then," Julia mused.

"What?" Jones said, sharply.

Julia blinked. The lack of sleep must have been worse than she'd realized, she hadn't meant to say that out loud. "Oh, sorry, it was just gossip. Someone was saying that he was a suspect when Aimiee originally went missing."

Jones had fixed her with a penetrating stare and Julia found herself squirming under it. She'd forgotten just how good he was at deploying silence when he needed to. "But obviously not, because you said there weren't any suspects," she said, fidgeting with her fingers as she spoke.

"Well, you're not entirely wrong, Lance was a suspect at the time. Of sorts," Jones said. "But I ruled him out fairly quickly, he had an alibi."

"But you told me before that there weren't any suspects," Julia said, suddenly feeling rather betrayed the inspector hadn't deemed it fit to share that with her.

"Well, it was to spare someone's blushes," Jones said.

"Lance's?"

Jones screwed his face up. "I'm not sure he has many blushes to spare. No, his alibi was one of the girls from Aimiee's year, so I didn't feel the need to broadcast it."

"Yuck," said Julia instinctively.

"Yes, quite," said Jones. "But at least he had the good grace to marry her."

"Oh," Julia said. She hadn't realized that Janice's relationship with the man had gone back quite that far.

"Yes, 'oh'," said Jones. "So you can cross Lance off the list of suspects that I'm sure you're keeping."

Julia looked forlornly at the ground and Jones's expression softened slightly.

"Anyway, Lance told me he was leaving town so you shouldn't have to worry about him showing up and causing trouble anymore."

Julia's eyes flickered to the ungainly stack of hay in the corner of the car park, wet and dripping with the morning's dew.

Jones swivelled his head to see what Julia was looking at.

"So what's that got to do with all this?" Jones asked, pointing at the hay.

Julia hesitated for a moment before replying, and in that instant Jones began striding over the stones towards the hay stack.

"I don't think it's anything really," Julia said. Obviously her ideas of Lance hiding bodies in there had been entirely fanciful. She blamed Sally for putting thoughts in her head.

But Jones wasn't listening. He approached the hay stack and reached forward to pull one of the bales aside. He gave a humourless laugh as he looked inside.

"More building work, is it?" Jones said, shaking his head. "Lance is involved with this, is he?"

Julia nodded meekly.

The sound of footsteps approaching made Julia turn and she saw Ivan hurrying over. He had a nervous grin spread across his face. "Rhys–" he began, but Jones cut him off.

"What is this, Ivan?" he demanded, stabbing a finger at the hay behind him.

"I just needed a hole dug," Ivan said.

The detective gave him a withering look. "Would this be related to that building work, by any chance?" He flashed a look in the direction of the building site in the beer garden.

"I did think maybe I could get a head start putting the septic tanks in," Ivan muttered.

Jones nodded thoughtfully. "You need planning permission for septic tanks, don't you?"

"Maybe in the strictest sense," said Ivan.

"And in the less strict sense?"

"In the less strict sense, I thought maybe I could plonk them in and no one would mind." Ivan sighed.

"Listen, and listen good," Jones said. "No more games with this building site, understood? It's bad enough in my opinion that they let you carry on when they found that poor girl's bones. But you've got no planning permission for this work and, I assume, no employment contract for Lance. From now on, you do everything by the book."

"Come on, Rhys," Ivan said.

"I mean it. I'll be keeping an eye on you."

"But you know what the council's like. Some biddy down the road will complain it will de-home a newt or something. The planning permission will take months."

"Then I'll keep my calendar clear," Jones said. "And what's more, when you see Lance, you tell him to make good on his promise and get lost."

Ivan scowled at Julia but before he could speak Jones answered his unasked question.

"No, I didn't hear it from her," Jones said. "Half the builders on your site know what's going on."

Ivan swallowed. "Fine. I'll tell Lance to move along. Without the work, I doubt he'd see much reason to stay anyway."

Julia couldn't help thinking of Janice in the cottage up on the hill, struggling to make ends meet.

"Good," Jones said, apparently the last word on the matter because he stalked away towards his car.

Julia looked up at Ivan, who had his vein throbbing on his forehead. "Sorry, Ivan," she said gently.

He did his best to smile. "Not your fault, Julia," he said. "Now come on, let's get ready to open."

* * *

Sally arrived an hour later to work the bar. With a quick glance around to make sure Ivan wasn't about, Julia hurried in to tell her about the morning's events. But before she got a chance, Sally leaned in and began speaking in a breathless whisper.

"Did you hear that they found Aimiee's bones?" Sally said.

"Yes–" Julia said, and Sally barrelled on.

"Can you believe she was shot?" Sally said.

"Shot!?" Julia gasped. No one got shot in places like Biddle Rhyne.

"Yes. Well, shot with an air rifle. So not shot shot. But still."

"Where did you hear this?" Julia asked.

"Charlie told me," said Sally. "But it's all over the news."

"Jones told me that the body was buried last night," Julia said. "It would have been when we were hiding in the hay stack."

Sally bit her lip thoughtfully. "That rules Lance out then, doesn't it?"

"Yes," Julia said. "And, speaking of, Jones found out what Lance was up to in that hay stack."

At that moment the staff door swung open and Ivan came through at his usual hurried pace. "Come on, girls," he said. "I don't pay you to chat."

Sally was looking pleadingly at Julia.

"Later," she mouthed, and hurried back to the dining room.

* * *

Exhausted, Julia finally made her way in through the front door and kicked her shoes off. The shift at the pub would have been knackering enough even if she hadn't been running on fumes. Sally was working the evening shift, so to make it worse Julia had needed to walk all the way back down the lane as well.

As she bent down to undo her shoes she caught sight of a note lying on the floor just on the edge of the doormat. She picked it up and flicked it open. Scrawled on a plain scrap of paper in a nearly illegible hand with blue ink were the words 'Mess with my livelihood and I'll mess with yours!'

Julia groaned. She could guess who had written the note. It seemed Jones and Ivan had been far too optimistic thinking Lance would just slink away with his tail between his legs.

Julia screwed the note up into a ball.

"Rumpkin?" she called.

The dog came trotting over to greet her, tongue hanging out. Julia gave the dog a playful pat on the head, already feeling slightly revived at the sight of his dopey face, and then threw the crumpled paper towards the bin in the corner, missing. She could call Jones once she'd got changed and make sure he chased Lance away properly.

It was dark up in her room with the curtains drawn. As she was reaching for the light switch her foot collided with something on the floor and she stumbled forward, losing her balance and ending up on her knees on the carpet.

Julia struggled upright, feeling something wrap around her ankle as she did so. She groped around on the wall for the light switch and blinked as the bulb came on.

Mark's stupid overnight bag lay on the floor, one strap caught around her foot. Anger rose inside her, the number of times she'd told him not to leave it lying just inside the door, it wasn't the first time she'd almost broken her neck tripping over it. She gave the bag a solid shove with her foot, pushing it into a corner of the room where it was out of the way. The zip was open and the bag left a trail of clothing behind it as it went.

Shaking her head, Julia stooped to pick up the clothes and chucked them in the general direction of the bag. But there was something else on the floor, hidden under the clothes – rubbish, by the looks of it, empty packaging of some sort. She picked it up.

Julia found she was holding packaging for a spy camera. The torn box advertised that the device was practically impossible to detect and could record for days at a time.

The room started to spin about her and her stomach felt sick.

Had Mark been spying on her? And if so, how long had he been up to it? She knew he'd been a bit jealous ever

132

since Charlie had given her that silly necklace he'd found, but she didn't realize Mark would sink that low. She hadn't thought that he had it in him.

She stood with the box in her hands for a few moments more, reading the sickening advertising.

She needed to ask him about this, and needed to do so right now.

Casting the box angrily aside, she pounded down the staircase to get her phone from her bag.

Just as she reached down to grab it, her phone it lit up. She picked it up and saw Mark was calling her.

Julia shivered. She hated it when that happened and she was in no mood at all to take such things in her stride right now.

Torn between anger and general unease, she jabbed the answer button with her finger. "What?" she snapped.

"Hi, Julia. Erm, I think you'd better get down to the shop. Right away if you can." Mark's voice seemed faint and wavering.

"Why?" Julia asked, unable to keep her anger up in the face of his obvious worry. "What's the matter?"

"It's probably best if you get down here," Mark said.

Chapter 14

Julia hurried out of the house and through the quiet evening streets to the shop.

A police car was just pulling up outside as she came into sight. As though she wasn't worried enough, her nerves kicked into overdrive and she could hear the blood pumping in her ears as she increased her pace.

The constable who stepped out of the car was discussing something with Mark at the foot of the old library steps when Julia arrived.

"What is it? What's happened?" Julia asked, her breath emerging in great white puffs.

Both Mark and the police officer looked at her with blank faces.

"Follow me," Mark said simply.

With that he turned and led the way up the short flight of stone steps, with Julia and the officer following.

As Julia stepped from the entrance hall into what would soon be the shop floor, her mouth fell open in horror.

"Oh, no," she whispered.

A trickle of red ran across the floor just in front of her toes, seeping into the carpet. At its head was an upturned paint can. That was only the start of the damage. The shelves fixed to the wall had been bashed in; some held together with splinters, others caved in entirely in the middle. The free-standing shelves had been pushed over, most of them breaking in the process. The books that had lined the shelves were strewn across the room, spines broken, and torn pages littered the whole scene. Overhead the lightbulb had been shattered, and small shards of broken glass glittered here and there in the light spilling in from the hallway.

Julia rotated slowly on the spot, taking in the scene of wanton destruction. They had been so close to finishing. So many hours of hard work that they had poured into this place, and it had been undone in a single, cruel act.

A car drove by on the high street, its headlamps lighting up the front windows of the shop just for an instant. Julia's gaze caught one of her 'Opening Soon' banners plastered there, mocking her.

Well, that was no longer the case, it seemed. Opening at the end of the month was out of the window now. Julia wondered grimly if the council would consider letting them delay. Mr Peabody's face drifted unbidden into her mind, and she realized it would be a lost cause. And besides, she and Mark barely had the money to stay afloat with their original timeline.

The policewoman spoke gently at her shoulder. "Any idea who might have done this?" she asked.

Julia couldn't answer straight away, she found herself transfixed by the smashed shelves and destroyed books in front of her. She shook herself out of it.

"Lance Teller," she said. "The police found out about his cash-in-hand work today, and I'm sure he blames me for that. When I got home there was a note. He didn't sign it but I'm pretty sure it was from him."

The constable's notebook had come out and she was scribbling notes down at a frantic pace.

"I'll pay Mr Teller a visit," the woman said, closing the book and looking around thoughtfully. "But I'm afraid to say that unless he was daft enough to remove something from the scene, it would be a difficult prosecution to make. There won't be much evidence it was him unless we have a witness come forward. I don't suppose the building has any CCTV?"

"No," said Julia.

"Yes," said Mark.

The policewoman raised one eyebrow and Julia shot Mark a look. "What?"

"Well, sort of," Mark said.

With that he crossed the room, picking his way carefully between the fallen shelves and the general debris. He clambered up onto the top of the counter. Julia winced as there was the sound of broken glass being crushed under the knees of his work trousers, but he didn't appear to notice.

He stood up with a slight wobble and reached to the light fixture above.

"It's still running," Mark said, unclipping something from behind the light.

He held whatever it was out between thumb and forefinger towards the two women, but it was barely discernible in the poor light. Realizing this, he jumped back off the counter and with long strides picked his way back over the floor to the doorway.

"Here," he said, holding his palm out.

Julia leaned in closely. "Spy cam," she said, eyeing the tiny black device that he held.

Mark nodded. "That's right."

"Don't think that I'm not glad, but why do you have that there?" Julia asked. "And why didn't you tell me?" She glared at him.

Mark's face turned apologetic. "I've seen too many building sites have all their tools nicked before," he said. "I thought the shop would probably be easy pickings. Normally, I just insure it all, but for such a small job it was hardly worth the cost.

"Sorry, Julia. I know how you worry about things; I didn't want to be putting thoughts in your head. You'd be seeing burglars everywhere if I told you. I've only turned it on at night when we're not around."

She scowled at him, but had to concede that he was probably right.

"Can we see what we've got?" the constable prompted.

Mark pushed at the spy cam with his thumb and a microSD card popped out. He slotted it into his phone and tapped a few buttons until an image appeared on the screen.

It was small and grainy but there was no doubt about it, it was undoubtedly Lance on the film. He appeared from behind the camera holding a crowbar and nonchalantly set to work, swinging wildly at the shelves, knocking the books off at random. At one point he turned to the light hiding the camera and Julia watched the crowbar arcing towards the screen. It was a small miracle the spy cam had come away undamaged.

Julia said some choice words about Lance as she watched him saunter back out the way he'd come, crowbar hanging at his side.

"I'd better go and pick Lance up," the officer said, a decided note of weariness in her voice as though she'd done this all before. "Can I take that?" she said to Mark.

Mark removed the SD card again and handed it over.

"Right," the woman said as her fist closed firmly around it. "I think I have everything I need. You two take care of yourselves."

They bade her goodbye and the policewoman let herself out of the shop leaving Mark and Julia to survey the damage.

"Well, that should be Lance taken care of for a good long while," Julia said. She gave a triumphant little 'hmph' and then, taking in the sight of her shop once more, she burst into tears.

Mark scooped her up in his arms.

Julia sniffed as she buried her head in Mark's shoulder. "I'm sorry I doubted you, Mark," she said.

"I didn't know that you did," Mark replied to the top of her head.

She pushed back a little and Mark looked down at her tear-stained face. "Don't worry," he said. "We'll get all this sorted out. You'll see."

Julia rummaged for a tissue and dabbed at her eyes. "You're a poor liar, Mark," she said.

To her disbelief, he gave Julia a wide grin. "I thought you trusted me now," he said.

Julia waved a hand about the room. "The carpets are ruined. And the shelves. And most of the stock. It's hopeless."

"Nah," Mark said, looking up and down. "A few new shelves. Most of the books will be fine. And look…" With an excessive amount of grunting, he squatted down and heaved one of the free-standing shelves back upright. "This one's okay," he declared.

He leaned into it with his shoulder and began to push, wheezing with the effort.

"What are you doing?" Julia asked.

"Mind out," he said.

Julia shuffled back as he edged the shelf along until it was covering up the spilled paint.

"There," Mark said, standing back with satisfaction to admire his work. "Now we don't have to worry about the carpet."

Julia scowled but the tears had stopped. "There's no room between the shelf and the counter," she pointed out.

"That's okay, it's cosy," Mark said. He sucked his stomach in and stepped into the tiny gap between the shelf. "It's fine."

Julia let out a deep huff. "Get out of there, Mark. You're probably trampling on evidence anyway."

Mark obliged and crabbed sideways out to join her. "Oh, no," he said, holding his palms to his face.

"What?" Julia's eyes darted around to see what further calamity she might have missed.

"The lightbulbs," Mark groaned. "Do you think we can afford to replace them?"

Julia laughed and held Mark in a deep hug. She held him for what seemed like a long time until someone cleared their throat noisily to get their attention.

Julia disentangled herself and saw Jones standing in the doorway, surveying the destruction.

"I came as soon as I heard," he said. He shook his head as he took the scene in. "Safe to assume this was Lance, then?"

"Definitely," Mark replied. "I caught him on a hidden camera."

Jones muttered darkly under his breath. "At least that's something. I'll bet he really has left town now, though."

"I wouldn't be so sure," Julia said.

Outside the shop window, Lance stood, hands on his hips and a huge grin across his face as he made a show of looking up and down at the wrecked building.

Seeing that he had everyone's attention, he strode casually round to the door and stepped inside.

"My, my," he said. "What a shame this is. And I do love a bookshop. Whoever would have done such a thing?"

Jones didn't waste any time. He grabbed Lance roughly by the shoulder to spin him around and began to place him under arrest.

"Hey," Lance protested. "You can't do this. You have no proof it's me."

"We have you on CCTV," Julia said triumphantly.

"No you don't," Lance said. "I made sure there weren't any cameras."

"I don't think that's the winning defence you think it is," Jones said as he clapped the handcuffs on.

* * *

When they got to the front door, Julia gave Mark a quick peck on the cheek and stepped inside.

It was late by now and Julia was tired and famished, but tiredness seemed to be winning out over hunger and bed was calling softly to her.

Rumpkin had other ideas. He ran, barking, towards her from the living room and made circuits of her ankles.

"Yes, yes, okay, I'll feed you," she huffed at the animal as she headed into the kitchen and set to opening a tin of food.

Julia's phone went off just as she was scraping the can out and she pulled it from her bag.

She had a message from Janice Teller.

'I hear you caught Lance,' she read.

'Yes – in police custody now', Julia texted back.

'Good.'

Julia yawned and plugged the phone in to charge by the kettle before leaving Rumpkin to his meal, although it sounded like he was already chasing an empty bowl around the floor. As she emerged from the kitchen, she was surprised to see Sally talking to Mark in the doorway, their heads close together as they whispered to one another.

Mark darted away just as Julia caught a glimpse of him, and Sally hastily shut the door after him.

"Was Mark still here?" Julia asked, hearing the confused tone in her voice.

"He was just saying goodbye," Sally said, and hurried away upstairs to her room.

Frowning, Julia followed her upstairs to her own room and began getting changed.

She was trying not to be suspicious of Mark, after it turned out the spy cam had a perfectly innocent explanation. But there was definitely something going on there.

Despite her worries, as soon as her head hit the pillow Julia fell asleep.

* * *

It was Sally who woke her, patting her roughly from outside the duvet.

Julia rolled over and moaned, trying to make sense of what was going on.

"What time is it?" Julia asked, trying to blink away the sleep from her eyes.

"Almost midday," Sally replied. Now that Julia could focus, Sally looked annoyingly refreshed and perky.

A groan escaped Julia's lips.

"You've slept all morning," Sally continued. "Not that I blame you, with everything that happened. But there's work to be done."

"Ivan called?" said Julia.

Sally smiled. "No, at the shop. Come on, get up."

Sally left her to it so Julia struggled out of bed and into some clothes, doing her best to run a brush through her hair before she went downstairs.

Relentless, Sally was waiting for her with a travel cup in her hand which she shoved towards Julia as she reached the hallway.

Julia took the cup, but grudgingly. It did admittedly smell like just what she needed, as much as she felt that she would be justified in heading straight to the armchair and crawling back under a blanket.

Sally thrust a coat towards Julia. "Come on," she said.

"What's the point? The shop's a wreck, we'll never get it sorted in time," she said, but she put her coat on all the same.

Sipping on the coffee, Julia followed Sally out to the car. Sally hit the button on the radio and some 1980s hits started flowing out.

"The shop's not far, we could have just walked," Julia said. If she wasn't quite able to bring herself to voice her insecurities about her friend and whatever was going on with Mark, she could at the very least subject her to a good moan.

"I thought we might need to take some of the damaged books away," Sally said.

"Oh, right." Julia slumped further down into the seat as she remembered the mental image of the ruined books, strewn all over the shop floor after Lance's rampage. "Those."

The parking bays down the side of the high street all seemed to be occupied, so Sally was forced to drive a bit further along and park on one of the side streets. As they walked back towards the shop, Julia wondered idly if there might be something on at the Fox and Hounds.

Turning the corner onto the high street, Julia heard the shop before she saw it. The sound of power tools and hammering rang out. Even in Julia's sleep-addled state she realized this was peculiar, as Mark tended to limit himself to using one tool at a time.

When they got inside the shop, Julia could only stand, blinking. The place was a hive of activity. Mark and Charlie were busy doing something useful-looking to the counter. She couldn't identify exactly what, but the counter itself seemed in much better nick than when she'd last seen it.

Several of the other builders she recognized from the Barley Mow were fixing shelves onto one of the walls; the wall opposite was already finished. All of the broken shelves and ruined books had been cleared out, leaving the middle of the room looking airy and spacious.

Charlie looked up as she entered, showing a toothy smile. "I did say that I wanted to help," he said, still working away with whatever tool he had on the countertop. Julia noticed a look pass between him and Sally.

Julia turned to her friend. "I take it you had a hand in this?" she said.

Sally gave an uncharacteristically modest shrug.

Julia took a step towards the counter and stopped, looking down at her feet. What had before been a ruined mess of paint was now lush and pristine carpet.

"How did you manage that?" Julia asked.

"That was me," a voice said from behind the counter. Janice's head popped into view.

"I never thought that paint would come out," Julia said.

"It didn't. There were still plenty of offcuts from the carpet, I just stitched them in. Lucky you and Mark are slow to clean up after yourselves, isn't it?"

"It's seamless," Julia said. She'd never been so excited by a carpet before. "I don't know what to say. Thank you so much."

"I know I'm not really responsible for the Idiot's actions" – Julia gathered that Janice meant Lance – "but I can't help feel that I am, sometimes."

"No, I mean it. Thank you. All of you," Julia said, raising her voice to address the whole shop.

A car horn sounded on the street just outside the window. A lorry from the brewery had pulled up. She knew it from its drop-offs at the Barley Mow, and it shouldn't have been coming down the high street. It definitely shouldn't have been parked alongside Mark's van, blocking the traffic in both directions down the road.

With a rattle, the back of the lorry was drawn up and a dolly was wheeled onto the tailgate.

"What?" Julia took a step closer for a better view.

It wasn't the usual stacks of metal barrels, but a towering, dark wood bookcase on the dolly, slowly descending to street level. A minute later the beleaguered-looking driver pushed the dolly into the shop, angling the load carefully to get it through the doorway, with Ivan striding in after him.

"That was a lot of steps. You didn't tell me anything about steps," the driver said. He did not look happy.

Ivan did, though. He turned his broadest smile onto Julia.

"Ivan," Julia said to him. "What on earth is this?"

The pub landlord slapped the side of the giant bookcase, oblivious to the fiery look the driver gave him as it wobbled precariously on the dolly.

"Bookshelves," he said proudly.

"I can see that," Julia said. "But where have they come from?"

"They belong to the pub," Ivan said. "Well, they did. Now they belong to you, I guess. They were there when I took over the place. I had them moved out of the common areas because kids kept trying to climb them. Including you, if I remember. But I've had no real use for them, I don't really read many books, I don't have the time."

Poor Ivan. No time to read books. That probably explained all his bad tempers. Julia stepped forward as the shelf was unloaded onto the carpet and she ran her finger over the rich wood. It was intricately carved, a delicate pattern criss-crossing around the shelves.

"I think it's properly old," Ivan said. "Probably twelve hundreds or something."

Julia rather doubted it was quite that old, but they were beautiful all the same.

"Thank you, Ivan," she said.

Ivan leaned close, not wanting to be overheard, although the rest of the room was making a show at being busy at their various tasks.

"I'm really sorry about how things went down, Julia," he said, the smile disappearing and suddenly looking serious. "If I'd known Lance was capable of this, of course I wouldn't have had him working for me. And I told him you had nothing to do with Jones finding out about that, but I guess he didn't believe me.

"Anyway. He won't be welcome in the Barley Mow again, I can tell you that much."

Julia stretched up on her tiptoes and gave her boss a quick hug. "Thanks, Ivan," she said again.

Mark had downed tools and sidled over. "Do I need to intervene here?" he said.

Julia slipped an arm around his waist. "Thank you for all this," she said to Mark.

A horn blared again outside and Ivan turned to the driver and his dolly. "You'd better get moving, mate. Three more to come and the traffic doesn't sound happy about waiting."

As the driver headed for the door, wheels of the dolly squeaking as he went, Julia took in the room in a slow circle.

It was looking like a shop. An empty shop, in terms of books rather than people, but a shop, nonetheless. It really was going to open.

Chapter 15

It was a cold morning and the damp hung in the air. Julia hurried along the lane, swaddled up in all her winter clothes so that little more than her nose was poking out.

After yesterday's huge collective effort, the bookshop was finally back on track, leaving her to mull over the case.

The whole episode with Aimiee's bones was mystifying Julia, and it had been going around in her mind the whole walk in.

Jones was right, it was almost like someone wanted them to be found. And it did seem like whoever had buried them had done so with respect.

But then why run off with them in the first place?

Her only guess was that Aimiee's dad might have got wind of the bones and got there before the police turned up because he didn't want his daughter languishing in a morgue while the investigation took place.

Julia couldn't blame him for wanting to finally give Aimiee some rest, but it seemed highly unlikely that Graham would have heard so quickly about the bones and made it to the Barley Mow between Julia finding them in the rhyne and Jones making it to the scene.

And then there was the fact Aimiee had been shot. Sally's gossip had been right, forensics had confirmed that Aimiee had been killed by an air rifle pellet to the side of the head.

An air rifle was hardly the most reliable of murder weapons. The shot that killed Aimiee had been incredibly lucky. Or unlucky, depending on the shooter's intentions, Julia supposed.

She did her best to push those thoughts away as she stepped through the door of the Barley Mow and started peeling her layers off before she began sweating. She was midway through unwinding her thick, woolly scarf when she made her way through to the kitchen and a smile lit up across her face.

"Rob," she said. "Nice to see you back!"

The chef looked up from the counter where he had ingredients spread out in front of him ready to chop. He looked, to be frank, awful. He was even paler than when Julia had last seen him.

"Hi, Julia," he intoned softly, his voice was dry and rasping.

Julia stood considering him for a moment. "Are you sure you're quite all right?" she asked him. "You look—" she scrambled for an adequate description that wouldn't sound grossly offensive "—not well."

Rob gave a slow shrug. "Maybe not. Ivan said if I wasn't back in today, he'd need to start looking for a replacement."

Julia's smile quickly moulded itself into a scowl. "I'll have a word with him," she said grimly.

Rob held up a hand to stop her. It looked like he'd been biting his nails. "Don't," he said. "It's fine, really. I can't hide myself away at the farm forever. It's probably for the best to get this over with."

"If you're sure," Julia said.

He gave a little nod and turned back to the vegetables on the counter, picking up the knife.

"Well, if you need anything, you'll tell me, won't you?" Julia said.

But Rob didn't reply, he was already set to his task, the knife rising and falling rhythmically on the chopping board.

* * *

After the builders had finished lunch, Julia turned down the dining room and then stuck her head into the kitchen but it was empty so she headed out through the parlour where Ivan stood behind the bar.

"Is Rob already gone?" she asked him.

Ivan inclined his head towards the door. "You just missed him," he said.

She couldn't resist a parting shot as she pulled her gloves on. "You shouldn't have hurried him back," she chided Ivan.

146

Ivan pulled a face. "The distraction will do him good; he was too worked up. It should get him out of his own head, at least."

Julia harrumphed quietly to herself and headed for the door.

"Be careful out there," Ivan called after her.

She gave him a puzzled look but as she lifted the catch and stepped out she found herself in a thick fog. She hadn't noticed it from the dining room but it had risen up and become so dense that she could hardly make out the pub's sign, barely twenty yards away.

"Oh," she muttered.

It was hazardous enough going down the lane at the best of times, the way some people drove, but with visibility like this it might be downright dangerous. At least it wasn't far to the pedestrian cut-through to Biddle Rhyne's residential streets where there was pavement and the traffic was far more sedate. There was nothing for it so she drew her coat tight about herself, tweaked her scarf up and headed off. The ingrained memory of doing the journey so many times kept her on the tarmac more than anything else; she was only too aware of the freezing rhyne lying unseen a few feet away, the mist curling on top of it. She shivered and pulled her phone out of her bag, turning the torch on and hoping it would give the drivers a fair chance to see her before they trundled merrily straight over the top of her.

A drawn-out groan floated in off the moorland. Maybe a bird or some livestock calling out. The moors didn't normally bother Julia, she walked alongside them every day, but there was something deeply unsettling about them today and she quickened her pace.

She had never truly believed Aimiee's ghost had been playing on the pub swings. Childish stories that they told themselves. But on a day like today, as the mist curled in great tendrils around her ankles, she could almost convince herself it had been real.

The church bell struck. The sound seemed detached and incredibly distant. Julia had just reached the turn-off for the cut-through when she saw a figure standing in the mist ahead of her. Little more than a shadow was discernible at first. But then a gust of wind blew, rustling the dead leaves in the hedgerows and just for a moment parting the fog ahead of her. The figure was standing still and Julia peered closer, wondering if she might have caught Rob up.

They had their back turned, whoever it was, staring out over the moor.

"Rob?" Julia ventured.

The figure twitched and then began to turn around. Slowly but with an unsettling smoothness.

Julia let out a scream.

There was no doubting it, Barry stood in the fog in front of her. He was white as a sheet and his eyes seemed dark and sunken. He seemed to look through her rather than at her. He took one shuffling step in Julia's direction but that was enough.

She turned, still screaming and ran as fast as she could down the cut-through.

There was a tug on her head and she felt something clutching at her but she struggled on. Cold air rushed over her as her hat was plucked from her head and she screamed again, stumbling over the uneven pavement as she fled.

* * *

Julia didn't stop running until she was home. Her hands were shaking so badly that she struggled to get the key into the lock, jabbing repeatedly at it and then dropping them with a clatter onto the doorstep. The door opened as she stood up from collecting them and she saw Sally illuminated in the doorway, a concerned frown on her face.

"Oh, goodness, chicken, what's wrong?" Sally asked, helping Julia into the house. She peered into the gloom to see if there was anyone behind her.

Julia pulled Sally back inside and slammed the door as quickly as she could, making the windows rattle. She stood quaking on the runner, looking wild and disarrayed.

Sally wrapped her up in a hug and made gentle soothing noises. "There, it's okay," she crooned. "Now come on, tell me what's wrong."

In a muffled voice, Julia spoke into her friend's jumper. "I saw... I saw..."

"Yes, what did you see?"

"I saw a ghost," Julia managed.

Sally stopped rubbing Julia's back and pushed her away so she could look at her. "You saw a ghost?" she said, one eyebrow arching questioningly.

Julia nodded and bit her lip.

"You know it's foggy out there, right?" Sally said.

"Yes, I know it's foggy out there!" Julia snapped back.

"I mean, are you sure that you didn't see some fog? It's very wispy."

"I didn't see wispy fog," said Julia. "It was a ghost."

"Okay," Sally said gently. "What did it look like, this ghost?"

Julia scowled. She could feel irritation creeping in. Partly at Sally and partly at herself. But at least it was replacing the abject terror.

"It was Barry's ghost," Julia said.

Sally's face softened further. "Ah, I see," she said. "Look, I think that's normal, after what you've been through. I could put some tea on," she suggested.

"I don't need tea," Julia said stonily. There would be time for that later. "I need you to believe me. I actually saw Barry out there in the mist."

"And you're sure that you actually saw Barry out there?" Sally asked.

Julia nodded. "It was definitely him."

149

"And they weren't a bit taller? And a bit paler? And their hair a bit thinner on top?"

Julia paused. She hadn't noticed the ghost's hair. "They were taller and paler," she said. That seemed pretty natural for a ghost, though, in her opinion.

"I think you might have seen Barry's older brother," Sally said, studying Julia's face for a reaction.

It didn't take a trained observer to spot it. Julia could feel herself blushing bright red. Of course it would be Terrence. He was barely more than a year older than Barry and he'd been the absolute spit of him growing up. She didn't think he'd been back in Biddle Rhyne since he'd turned eighteen but it made sense with his younger brother being killed that he'd come and spend time with his parents.

Julia hung her head. "Probably," she whispered.

Sally gave a lopsided smile. "Shall we have that tea now?" she suggested.

"No," Julia said. She smoothed her hair down. "I just need to pop out for something."

She reached for the door.

"Julia?" she said.

"Yes?" she replied, one hand on the handle.

"Are you going out to check for ghosts?"

Julia paused before replying. "Maybe," she said, quickly slipping back out into the fog.

* * *

First, Julia headed back the way she had come. The village was built on a slight rise in the flat landscape of the moors and the fog was relatively thin across the residential streets.

As she started to approach the lane and the road sloped downwards, the fog began to thicken, curling around the street lamps that were starting to flicker on. Despite Sally's explanation of the supposed ghost, Julia still felt her heart beating a little faster and part of her regretted setting off on this task, when she could be safely at home with tea brewing in the pot. But she was here now and she knew she wouldn't forgive herself for her cowardice if she turned back. And Sally would probably mock her relentlessly.

She arrived at the cut-through between the two high wooden fences that led out onto the lane. A dark shape bobbed in the alleyway, apparently floating in the air just above head height.

Cautiously, Julia crept forward, wishing that there was someone else around. The village seemed oddly deserted today. Most people had better sense than to be out in this weather, she supposed.

Swaying just above her was the woolly hat that she had felt being snatched off her head as she ran. It was snagged on one of the brambles that perennially overhung the alleyway, encroaching from the poorly tended garden on the other side of the fence. Julia gave it a rueful look as it bobbed and swayed in the breeze. She reached up and plucked the hat from the thorns, teasing it away as gently as she could. It still came away with strands of wool unravelled at the top.

"Drat," she said, turning it over in her hands to inspect it before pulling it down over her head.

She carried on through the alleyway and stopped at the lane, the curling white mist so thick it obscured the other side. A car sped past, unseen until it was almost upon her, reminding her just what a stupid idea it was that she'd embarked on. Julia peered left and right fruitlessly. She wasn't sure exactly what she had been expecting. That Terrence would just be standing around here still, loitering in the mist for no reason?

At any rate, there weren't many places that Terrence could have gone. Julia quickly ruled out the possibility that he was off to take a stroll over the moors given the weather. That probably ruled out walking up Pagan's Hill, too, there wasn't going to be much of a view up there today. Despite fleeing at full speed, Julia was fairly certain she would have noticed if she'd been followed down the cut-through earlier, so that only really left two directions. The Barley Mow one way down the lane and the village in the other.

She definitely didn't fancy another walk down the lane to the pub and anyway, Ivan could tell her tomorrow if Terrence had shown up there, so she turned in the other direction up the lane. It was only a short section of road to navigate in the fog and then she'd be back on pavements and feel a bit safer. She dimly remembered that Terrence and Barry's parents' street was only a little way along the high street, so that seemed a sensible bet.

Julia managed to reach it without encountering another ghost or another car. It was a small winding cul-de-sac of semi-detached homes. Lights shone rosily from several of them, creating glowing patches in the fog. Julia stood at the turn-off peering up the street before heading up, trying to remember which was the right house. It was years since she'd been up this street and it was peculiar seeing it again, especially in such an eerie setting.

She came to a halt just a couple of doors down outside a house which, somewhere deep in her memory, rang a bell and she looked over the low hedges trying to decide if she should go and knock on the door. She was saved from making a decision when the light flicked on in the front room and a man stepped into view, apparently freshly showered because he was wearing a thick, brown dressing gown, rubbing a towel over the top of his head. Julia knew she was behaving rather indecently, lurking in the bushes and peering in the windows, but for a moment she couldn't tear herself away.

It was uncanny just how like his late brother Terrence was. Even now, if Sally hadn't reminded her about Terrence she would have sworn up and down that she was looking at Barry. But it was true, now that she looked properly, without the mist and, frankly, her hysterics, there were differences. A slight difference in height, and in the way he held himself. The brow was slightly higher and deeper set, making his eyes seem darker. And, yes, as he flung the towel over the back of a chair, Julia could see that his hair was a bit thinner on top, too.

Terrence began to turn in Julia's direction and she quickly hurried on up the street, shaking herself out of her little trance and chiding herself for being so daft earlier. Of course, upon reaching the end of the cul-de-sac she found herself standing with nowhere to go so she turned and, with her scarf pulled up around her face against the cold, went back the way she came.

Chapter 16

Unable to sleep, Julia had risen early, before the sun was up. She had the morning to herself. She wasn't due at work until almost noon and Mark had declined her offer to help at the shop. Thanks to everyone's heroic efforts righting Lance's destruction, there were only a few finishing touches to go now: a couple of shelves and bits of signage to attach. Mark had given her strict instructions to stay away so he could keep the final presentation a surprise.

The plan had been to finally catch up on some of her reading, which had gone neglected during the renovations. But with the grand opening mere days away, she found herself wholly unable to think about much else. She wondered, not for the first time, if she'd get away with sneaking a peek at Mark's final adjustments.

Rumpkin came in, apparently finished with his investigation of the kitchen, clambered up into Julia's lap and put his paws on her chest and his nose into her face. She looked at the dog's face, difficult given it was only an inch away from her own, and did her best to avoid his tongue as it came flickering out towards her mouth.

"Fine," she said, "I'll take you for a walk." At least being out on the moors would remove the temptation to go and interfere with the work at the bookshop.

Hearing the W-word, Rumpkin ran off towards the front door.

After speaking briefly to the pile of duvet that may or may not have contained Sally, Julia decided she was allowed to take the car for the morning, or at least wasn't not allowed. So she put on her walking clothes and grabbed Rumpkin's lead. As soon as the front door was open, Rumpkin bounded out and put his front feet up onto the boot of the car.

"Yes, yes." Julia sighed, fumbling to unlock the car with her gloves on. "Just hang on."

The sun was creeping up now and yesterday's fog had cleared. In fact the morning dawned bright and sunny, but also cold. Frost still lingered on the ground wherever the sun had yet to reach. The high street was almost empty as she drove down. Rumpkin yipped away from the car's boot, his excited face occasionally popping up into view when he put his front paws up on the back of the middle seat. Watching him in the rear-view mirror, Julia couldn't help but smile at the creature.

Normally at this time there would be a steady stream of traffic heading the other way towards King's Barrow. Today, Julia seemed to have the road to herself, not that she was going to complain. Of course, the one car she did encounter going the other way was just outside the bookshop where Mark's van was parked at an angle, jutting out onto the street, and she was forced to sit behind the van waiting for the car to pass.

"He really needs to park that thing better," Julia said to herself, but really she was quite pleased to see that he'd made an early start. She had a peer-in through the shop windows while she waited, looking for Mark, but with the rising sun glinting on the glass she couldn't see in properly.

When the road cleared, Julia drove the rest of the high street, going cautiously as she always did now, then taking the right turn onto the lane. She had only been driving for about a minute when she saw something on the road ahead and swore under her breath. A line of blue and white police tape stretched across the lane, blocking access. Well, that explained the lack of traffic coming the other direction at any rate; probably some careless driver had driven themselves into the rhyne in yesterday's fog. It happened from time to time. If one of the local farmers found them first they could usually haul them out before the police got involved and shut the whole road down while they did whatever they did.

Julia pulled the car in on one of the narrow concrete bridges that served as field entrances and killed the engine. She wiped the moisture from the windscreen and squinted through, trying to see what was going on. Standing in front of the tape, Julia recognized the policewoman who had attended the break-in at the shop. She stood perfectly immobile as the tape danced behind her in the wind, looking very cold as well as rather bored. There was also a large man in a thick coat slightly to one side of the constable. He was also wearing a warm-looking hat with earmuffs and stood with his back to Julia, watching whatever activity was going on further down the lane. Julia strained her eyes looking but, aside from the suggestion of some flashing blue lights, she couldn't see anything.

With a beleaguered sigh, Julia pushed the car door open and stepped out, the cold air instantly making her wince and she pulled her scarf up. She walked briskly down the lane towards the tape, with the high hedgerow speckled with frost on one side, and the still water of the rhyne on the other. She rubbed her hands together as she went, trying to get some warmth into them.

The policewoman stood as still as a statue as Julia approached. How she did it in this weather was a mystery, she must have had ice in her veins.

The woman watched Julia approach, giving the smallest incline of the head in recognition. "Ma'am," she greeted Julia, her tone clipped but not unkind.

The large man also turned to say hello and Julia found herself standing next to Mortimer, the bird watcher. He was swaddled up well against the elements, his bulky black binoculars hanging as ever from around his neck. He gave Julia a little greeting and then went back to studying the scene taking place beyond the police line.

"What's going on?" Julia asked the police officer.

Julia tried to look over the woman's shoulder to further down the lane. There was a bustle of activity there. She could see a couple of police vehicles parked with their lights on and a handful of officers, in and out of uniform, milling around. She thought that maybe she could see the white uniforms of some forensic technicians. But beyond that, she couldn't see what had happened. It certainly wasn't the beached car that she had been expecting, though.

"There's been an incident," the policewoman said informatively. She stood unflinching; her face gave nothing away.

"So I see," said Julia. "What happened exactly?"

"I'm afraid I can't say," the officer replied.

Julia admitted defeat and was about to trudge back up the lane to the car, but then Mortimer jerked to attention, whisking his binoculars up to his face.

"It's our Rob!" he said.

"What?" Julia gasped. She gawked down the lane but from this distance she could only make out the vaguest of shapes. The white-clad forensic team did seem to be pulling something about person-sized from the rhyne, though.

Mortimer with his binoculars could obviously see more. He had them clamped over his eyes now and was bouncing up and down on his heels, struggling to restrain his excitement. The policewoman sidestepped in front of him, trying to obscure his view, but it was a futile effort. Mortimer just leaned with his hips and watched around her.

"They're pulling Rob out. I mean, they're pulling his body out," Mortimer said, the words tumbling from his mouth so fast that he was almost tripping over them.

The policewoman batted her hand at the offending binoculars but without missing a beat Mortimer sidled backwards out of her grasp.

"Oh, God," Julia said, staring in the direction of the grim scene, the cold suddenly forgotten.

"Maybe he fell in," Mortimer suggested.

"Maybe," Julia replied automatically.

"He must have been there a while," Mortimer continued, oblivious to Julia's distress. "They'd have got him out sooner if they thought he might still be alive. Perhaps he's been there all night long."

Julia shuddered. He might well have fallen in on his way home from work. If that was true, she could have walked right past him in the fog, not knowing he lay dead in the water just a few feet beside her. She bit her bottom lip. If only he had waited for her to finish, they could have walked back together and kept each other safe.

With those thoughts chilling her mind and the winter air chilling her body, she mumbled a quick goodbye to Mortimer and departed the way she had come, the outline of Pagan's Hill rising dark from the fields in front of her. Julia held a hand up to her face, shielding her eyes from the glare of the rising sun, and kept her gaze down. She had only made it about a dozen paces when she spotted something floating in the water of the ditch beside her. She crouched down in the thin strip of grass that separated the water from the tarmac, trying to get a better look. It was a jagged white shape drifting slowly along on the surface, disturbing the thick layer of green algae. Julia squinted at it – a sheet of paper, maybe?

Julia pulled a glove off and reached for it but the paper, or whatever it was, stayed frustratingly just beyond her grasp. She inched her weight forward, conscious that she didn't want to overbalance and end up in the water herself, and just managed to brush it with her fingertips. It was definitely a page of paper; the soggy material was cold against her skin and she fought the urge to recoil.

A shadow appeared from behind her, blocking her light, as someone loomed over. Before she had a chance to turn, the person leaned right over the top of her and with their long arms they plucked the page straight from the water. With a slight wobble, Julia managed to regain her balance, one hand groping the grass for stability, and then stood back upright again, turning as she did so.

She found Mortimer there, the dripping page held up to his face. "What do we have here?" he asked aloud, apparently more to himself than to Julia.

Julia edged around the man so she could see over his shoulder. It was indeed a piece of paper, a handwritten note on a page of A4. The ink had run in the water, dark streaks flowing down the page, but it was still legible.

> *I killed Aimiee and I am so sorry I never said anything before*
> *Tell dad I am so sorry*
> *Robert*

"Oh, gosh," Mortimer said, eyes squinting as he read the dripping note. "Oh gosh, oh gosh, oh gosh."

In fairness, although Mortimer was no wordsmith, the man's thoughts largely echoed Julia's own.

Mortimer swivelled his head to look at the police officer, who still stood stiffly to attention at the cordon.

"I'd better let her see this," Mortimer said.

Julia nodded her agreement and Mortimer padded off down the lane, binoculars swinging from their strap as he walked, the delicate note clutched carefully but firmly in both hands.

"I say there, miss, hello," he called to the constable as he went.

Julia turned away and walked, slightly stunned, back to the car. Poor Rob. She couldn't even imagine living with that kind of weight around his neck for all those years, but still she felt queasy in her stomach at the thought of him killing himself like that. And just after she'd seen him as well. She couldn't help but wonder if there was something she could have said when she saw him at the pub. Or maybe she and Sally should have made more of an effort to see him while he was off work?

She unlocked the car and slid into the relative warmth inside. Rumpkin barked manically at her. Doing her best to push her dark thoughts about Rob to one side, she put an elbow over the back of her seat so she could face the dog. "Guess we'll need to try the other direction for our walk," she said.

Rumpkin barked his agreement and Julia started the car, carefully making a three-point turn across the narrow lane, wary of the sudden drop into the rhyne's bank if she overshot. Once she was successfully facing the other way she drove on, past the high street, taking the lane in the opposite direction from the Barley Mow and up the side of Pagan's Hill.

* * *

The car was nicely warmed-up and only gave a token groan of protest as Julia drove it up the steep incline of the hill, pulling up in the broad sweep of mud and gravel that served as a parking area. Rumpkin sprang out of the boot as soon as it was opened and darted off along his familiar route, wriggling underneath the fence by the kissing gate

159

and disappearing into the woodland. Julia followed after him, pulling her coat and hat on as she went.

When they emerged out of the woods, the countryside was laid out before them, bathed in the morning light. The drainage rhynes crossed the fields like veins. The only landmarks in the flat marshes were little stone church spires, each one representing its own little community. Julia did her best to concentrate on the view and not the horrible discovery the police had made.

As she rounded a bend in the path, Julia found that she wasn't the only one out that morning. Janice Teller was sitting on the trunk of a fallen tree, legs dangling against the bark, gazing out over the top of her own plot of land to the scenery beyond. Rumpkin charged up and began jumping at her ankles, barking. Janice laughed and slid down to greet him, almost landing on top of the hapless creature but managing to just avoid him.

"Hello, Janice," Julia called.

When Janice straightened up from petting Rumpkin she gave Julia a worried look. "Julia, you look dreadful, love. Is everything okay?" she said.

"No, not really," Julia sighed.

She started to tell Janice about Rob and about the note that he'd left, confessing to Aimiee's killing.

Janice listened attentively, chewing on her fingernails throughout. When Julia finished, she couldn't help noticing that the other woman's fingers were bitten and raw, she'd obviously been in the habit for a while.

"Oh, poor Rob," Janice said. She looked out again over the moors below. "He seemed like such a nice chap. It's hard to imagine him doing such an awful thing, isn't it?"

"Yes," Julia agreed.

"I guess it just goes to show that you never really know someone," Janice said. "Actually, it's a really strange coincidence. I don't think I've spoken to him in years, but I was going to go and see Rob later today."

Julia gave her a questioning look and Janice continued. "I found something of his," she said. "Or, at least, I think it was his. Do you remember those pots I sold to the Barley Mow?"

Julia nodded. How could she forget? "The ones that Lance took," she said.

"The ones that Lance stole," Janice corrected. "Anyway, the police finally returned them to me yesterday. All the plants were dead. I think they'd just been in the back of Lance's car since he took them.

"So I emptied the pots out and I found a little metal heart in the bottom of one with Rob's name inscribed on it. Well, I don't know if it's the same Rob, but he's the only one I know and he works at the Barley Mow so I can't think how else it would have gotten into the bottom of one of the plant pots. Although why he'd put it there, heaven only knows."

Julia's mind flashed back to the day the pots had been delivered. She'd spent a good half an hour with the wheelbarrow and spade filling them with soil before planting Ivan's spruce trees in them. "I know how it got there," she said.

Janice looked at her. "Well, do tell."

"It was in the soil," Julia said. "That topsoil came from the mound the builders dug out. They already found a heart-shaped pendant when they were digging. I'll bet the metal heart you found was part of it, too. Can you show it to me?"

"Of course," Janice replied.

They set off downhill towards Janice's cottage. As they walked, Julia noticed Janice constantly fidgeting with her fingers, often raising them to her mouth and forcing them back away. As they arrived at the cottage, Julia realized what Janice was doing. She was fighting off the urge for a cigarette. Possibly kicking the habit was due to her lack of finances more than anything else, and not for the first time Julia felt a pang of sorrow for Janice.

Outside the cottage was a stack of ceramic pots, just as there had been on Julia's previous visit. The four that had briefly adorned the Barley Mow were sitting just off to one side, upturned. Janice went over and picked a tiny piece of metal off the top of one of them between thumb and forefinger and held it out towards Julia.

"I think this must be the front piece for the pendant we found," Julia said, thinking of the heart-shaped necklace that Charlie, in a roundabout way, had given to Sally. It was certainly the right size. It appeared that originally it would have been joined on with a hinge to form a locket.

She held it into the light and squinted. There was some writing inscribed on it, although it was worn and faded now.

"'Love from Rob'," Julia read.

Janice tapped the very top of the heart with her fingernail, or what was left of it. "There was some more writing here. Saying who it was to, I suppose. But it's worn away now, I can't read it."

"No," Julia said. "But I can guess. I think this was Aimiee West's pendant."

Janice's hands flew up to her face. "Oh, goodness, yes that does make sense," she said. "They found her body near there, too, didn't they? The poor mite."

Julia nodded. "I wonder if Aimiee's Facebook page still exists. We might be able to find some pictures of her wearing the necklace."

She pulled her phone out and tapped away. It wasn't long before she had found Aimiee's page.

It was chilling to see the young girl looking back at her, a face she hadn't seen for so many years. The page had remained untouched, of course, since shortly after she disappeared. There were a few messages wishing her well or asking her to contact them, and then further down was a stream of photos she had posted, dating from not long before she went missing.

"There!" Janice said, pointing at the phone screen.

The photo was small and grainy and Julia's attempts to enlarge it didn't really help. But just about discernible in the jumble of pixels was a little heart-shaped necklace around Aimiee's neck.

Julia and Janice looked at one another. "I think that more or less proves it," Janice said.

"Yes," Julia agreed.

"We should take it to the police," Janice said.

"Yes," Julia said. "I can do that."

She bade Janice goodbye, retrieved Rumpkin from the hedge he was exploring, and began off again in the direction of the car.

She called Jones as she walked.

"Julia," his voice greeted her. "What's up?"

Julia told him quickly about the locket. "I'm heading down the hill now," she said. "Where can I meet you?"

"I'm just at your bookshop right now," Jones said.

Julia paused midstride. "Why, what's happened?"

"Nothing's happened." Julia could hear Jones roll his eyes down the phone line. "I'm on my coffee break, that's all. I thought I'd lend a hand with the repairs."

Julia let out a sigh of relief and resumed walking.

"I'll be there in ten minutes," she said, hurrying her pace.

Chapter 17

Unlike Mark, Julia lived in more or less constant fear of the traffic warden's wrath and followed the rules of the double yellow lines rigidly. Accordingly, she drove a little past the shop and pulled up in one of the parking bays.

She looked at Rumpkin in the rear-view mirror. He looked back, his tongue hanging out.

"You can stay here for this one," Julia said.

She ignored the dog's whine as she got out of the car without him and, checking the front of the locket was still safely in her pocket, she walked briskly up the high street towards the shop. A couple of hours ago, she would have relished seeing the finishing touches Mark was making to the shop. Now, with her thoughts on Rob and the locket, her step felt heavy as she approached.

She squeezed by Mark's van and up the steps to the bookshop where she found Mark and Sally were hard at work on the shelves. Jones was less hard at work and apparently more there in a supervisory role, helping them to get one of the long shelves level on the wall.

There were three empty coffee cups from the café up the road on the counter next to Sally's handbag. It seemed they had made a nice morning of it and for a moment Julia felt a pang at being excluded. That wasn't fair, though. Mark had been keen to present the finished shop as a surprise – something Julia had now ruined by charging in – and besides, Jones would have been attending to Rob's suicide earlier on. Hardly a pleasant way to pass the morning.

As the shelf slotted into place and got Jones's seal of approval, the three of them turned to greet Julia. She pulled the metal heart from her pocket and held it out towards the inspector.

Jones produced an evidence bag from his suit and deftly wrapped the little heart up. Julia wondered if he carried those around with him all the time.

"How are you faring, Julia?" he asked as he squirrelled the evidence away.

"Not great," Julia admitted. "I suppose he did some nasty things. But his suicide? It's just terrible."

Sally gave a frown and wrapped herself around Julia.

Jones rubbed the bristles of his moustache with his knuckle. "I'm not so sure," he said.

Julia blinked at him. He was colder than she realized. "You don't think it's terrible?"

Jones shook his head. "I mean I'm not sure it's suicide."

"Oh," Julia replied, taking a moment for that to sink in. "Why not?"

Jones held his hands in front of him and began counting off on his fingers. "For one there's the note. I reckon it's potentially a fake. I'm told the handwriting matches Rob's, certainly the signature looks like the one on his credit card. But there are ways to forge that. Unfortunately since it's been in the water for so long I don't think we'll ever be able to tell. And the sign-off; he says goodbye to his dad. And only his dad. He's been staying with both his parents since Barry was killed."

Julia nodded. Hardly conclusive but it did seem a bit peculiar.

The inspector uncurled another finger and carried on. "Then there's the blow to the side of his head."

"What?" Julia exclaimed. "What blow?"

"Right," Jones said. "I forgot you wouldn't know about that. We had a look at Rob's body once we pulled him out of the water. He had a big bruise on the side of his forehead." Jones pointed to his own head, just above his eyebrow.

"You mean someone hit him?" Julia asked.

"It doesn't prove much either way," said Jones. "Someone could have hit him. But it's certainly still plausible that he sustained it when he threw himself into the rhyne. Caught a rock on the way down or something like that. But I don't like how it looks."

Jones ticked off another finger. "And finally, if you were going to kill yourself, why throw yourself into that rhyne, of all places?"

Julia nodded. "I know it's been done before," she said, although she could see the detective's point.

"I know," Jones said. "But the thing is only about five foot deep. There are simpler ways, I'm sure."

"And if it wasn't suicide?" Julia said.

Jones didn't have to say it, but he nodded. "It's a possibility I have to explore."

"And if the note was fake, then presumably you don't think Rob killed Aimiee?" Julia said.

"Again, I can't be sure," said Jones. He tapped his suit pocket. "If the note was forged, then it would follow that someone was framing him for it. That was my line of reasoning before you called.

"But it certainly seems like he gave this necklace to Aimiee, and when I interviewed him at the time of her disappearance, he said he barely knew her. We had no reason to doubt him back then, but now it certainly looks like he was lying to us."

Quiet descended on the shop as they all mulled the equally distasteful possibilities. Either Rob had killed Aimiee and then, all these years afterwards, killed himself, or Aimiee's killer was still out there somewhere and had murdered Rob, trying to frame him in the process.

Eventually Sally broke the silence. "Do you have everything you need from me?" she said to Jones. "I should really go and get ready for work."

"I've got your statement; you can head off if you want. I'll need to take Julia's," he said.

Sally gave her friend another quick hug. "Are you going to be all right?" she asked.

Julia glanced quickly over her shoulder to Mark who gave her a reassuring smile. "I'll be okay," she told Sally, "and you?"

Sally nodded and Julia handed over the car keys. "I'll be there in an hour or two, anyway. See you later."

As the door clicked shut, the inspector pulled his notebook out. "I'll need to hear everything you know about that necklace," he said. "Are you okay to do this now or do you need a moment?"

But Julia wasn't listening. She was staring off into space, her mind racing, thinking back to the events in the fog the day before.

Just what had Terrence been doing down the lane yesterday? Julia asked herself. She hadn't given it much reflection the previous day, she'd been so shaken by seeing Barry's ghost, as she had thought at the time. But now, in the very cold light of day, she had to wonder.

It didn't seem that he'd gone down to the Barley Mow, because she hadn't seen him there before leaving work. And by the time she went back out to reassure herself it was Terrence she saw and not Barry's phantom, barely fifteen minutes later, he was back at his house. It would be a stretch for Terrence to get to the pub and then back home in that time, let alone get a drink in as well. And given where Terrence's parents lived, there wasn't any reason he would use the cut-through into the lane, he would have taken the much simpler route along the streets that didn't involve looping out of the village. And since the whole moor was blanketed in the choking fog, it also seemed highly unlikely that Terrence would have been out enjoying the view.

"Julia?" Jones prompted.

"I think Rob was murdered," Julia said. "And I think that Terrence was the one who killed him."

Jones's eyes narrowed. "And why do you think that, exactly?" he asked her.

"I saw him on the lane yesterday, after work," Julia said. "I left work just after Rob, I was trying to catch him up, so Rob must have been there just a few minutes before."

"Okay," Jones said, noting that down in his pad. "So you can put Terrence at the place where Rob's body was found, around the time that he died. You didn't see him attack Rob, though?" He tapped his teeth thoughtfully with his pen.

"No, although he would certainly be big enough to overpower Rob," Julia said.

"And what motive would he have to kill Rob?" Jones said.

"I don't know," Julia conceded. "Perhaps Rob killed Barry and then Terrence found out?"

"Same question then," Jones said. "What motive would Rob have to kill Barry?"

Julia wracked her brains. Rob had seemed massively on edge after Barry's death. Far more so than she would have expected from mere colleagues at the pub. But she couldn't think of a reason for them to have fought.

"I don't know that either," she said. "There's all sorts of petty things they might have argued over." She refrained from adding that Barry had a way of getting under people's skin. "And Barry would certainly have let Rob into his flat. You said he was likely killed by someone he knew."

"Rob killing Barry. Well, it's a possibility," Jones said, although he sounded far from convinced. "Rob was never under particular suspicion so we never traced his movements the night Barry died." He flipped back through his notebook thoughtfully.

"So is what Julia saw enough to arrest Terrence?" Mark asked.

"Probably," Jones said. "But I'm not sure we could hold him on that. It's too circumstantial. And the note really weakens our case. Even if we think it was forged, his lawyer will surely argue that it wasn't."

Julia sighed. Maybe she was wrong about it all. It seemed flimsy now that she'd said it, and certainly she never would have thought Rob would be capable of killing Barry, so what motive would Terrence have had to kill Rob? She hoped that she hadn't set the inspector on the trail of an innocent man. She knew all too well what that felt like and she wouldn't wish it upon anyone.

Jones folded the notebook up and posted it away again. He did his best to give Julia a reassuring smile, not that it was hugely effective.

"Or what if Terrence killed his brother?" Mark asked. "If Rob found out, or suspected, then maybe Terrence killed him to keep him quiet."

"Nope," Jones replied quickly. "Terrence was at home in Manchester when Barry was killed."

"Do you know that for sure?" Julia asked.

"Yes, I checked on day one," Jones replied. "You don't have to look so surprised, it's my job."

"But he wasn't even a suspect," said Julia.

"Family are always suspicious," Jones said. He looked at Mark. "Sorry, Son."

Jones turned his attention to Julia. "You know, I can take your statement about the necklace later when you've had time to think this through," he said. "Right now, I need to get in touch with Mr West anyway. Regardless of whether I think that note is genuine or not, I have to inform him that we have a suspect for his daughter's murder."

Julia sighed at the thought. Not that she would want to trade places, but she didn't think this was an area where Jones's self-confessed old-school, matey style of police work was the best approach. The gruff old inspector might have a heart of gold underneath but he still lacked tact, and poor Mr West would undoubtedly be strung tight as wire.

"Just don't take him out drinking, Rhys. I know you mean well, but I don't think it's appropriate," Julia said.

Jones scratched his moustache and stared off into space. Julia thought he was going to ignore her entirely. But then he suddenly turned to look at her, pushing his suit jacket back to place his hands on his hips.

"What are you on about, Julia? Why would I take him drinking?" he asked.

Julia rolled her eyes and shifted in the chair. "I mean last time when you talked to him you took him to the Barley Mow. I know your heart was in the right place but, like I said, I don't think it's appropriate for someone grieving, that's all."

"Who told you that?" said Jones.

Julia frowned up at him. "No one told me. I was with you in the field when he arrived, remember? I saw him go off with you in your car."

"And I took Mr West back to the police station. I gave him a coffee from the machine," Jones finished for her.

"Oh," Julia was a bit stumped. "But Ivan said that Mr West had been in the pub. I just assumed it would have been then."

Jones shook his head at her slowly. "I took him to the police station and then I put him on a train home afterwards," he said.

"A train? But I thought he drove down," Julia said.

"He was in no state to drive back," replied Jones.

Julia had to agree there. Understandably, the man had been a wreck. He wouldn't have been safe behind the wheel. It was probably a small miracle that he'd made it down without an accident.

"What happened to his car?" Julia asked.

"It was only a hire car, I had one of the uniforms take it back to the local branch," Jones told her.

Julia drummed her fingers on the arm of her chair thoughtfully. "Don't call Mr West. Let me call Ivan first," she said.

She hoisted her handbag onto the shop counter and began rummaging through it. She could feel them both watching her intently as she did so. The blasted thing seemed to be able to hide when it wanted to. Eventually she managed to locate it and she pulled it free, spilling some throat sweets onto the floor of the shop as she did so.

The phone rang for what seemed an abominably long time before Ivan picked up.

"Julia," his voice said. "Please don't tell me you're calling in sick. I'm short-staffed as it is."

Julia scowled at the phone. That was one consequence of Rob's death, she supposed. It hadn't occurred to her that Ivan would be the real victim.

She managed to keep a lid on her temper, in light of Ivan's generous donation of the bookcases earlier that week. "Listen, this is important. Do you remember telling me that Mr West was in the pub the other day?" Julia said.

"As in Graham, Aimiee's father? Yes, I remember."

"Good," Julia replied. "And do you remember what day he was in?"

"Yes," Ivan said. "It was the day after the building work started."

Julia suppressed the urge to yell down the telephone line at him. Of course Ivan would remember it as the day after his precious building work started, and not the day that Barry was murdered. He might have helped connect the dots a bit faster if he had. She took a deep breath and spoke in a calm voice. "Thank you, Ivan. And do you happen to remember what car he was driving?"

She heard a long, strained sigh come from the phone. "No, I didn't really pay attention to that particular detail. Shall I look up who was on valet parking duty that day? Maybe ask them?"

Julia's patience finally wore thin. "There was no need for that, Ivan," she said and with great pleasure she hung up on her boss and dropped her phone back into her handbag.

She looked up at Jones and Mark. "It seems Mr West was in town the day that Barry died," she said. "Ivan doesn't know what car he was driving, but I'll bet good money that it was a white Micra. If I had good money, that is."

Jones began to pace up and down the narrow confines of the bookshop. "But I don't understand," he muttered. "Why would Mr West want to kill Barry? He can't have had anything to do with Aimiee's murder. He was out of the country at the time. With me."

"Can you just check what car he owns, first?" Julia asked. She didn't want to start throwing accusations about a man who had gone through everything that Mr West had. Falsely accusing one person of murder in a morning would be bad enough.

Jones fixed her a look. "If you know something..." he said.

"Please," Julia said. "You can do that, can't you? Look it up in the special police database, or something?"

"The special police database?" The inspector made a scoffing noise in the back of his throat and Julia felt herself reddening slightly.

"There is a database, but there are rules about accessing it. Procedures to be followed," Jones said. "It all takes quite a bit of time."

"Oh," Julia deflated a bit.

"However," Jones said. "You don't get to be a cop as long as I have without making a few useful contacts here and there. I've got a friend at the DVLA who could find out for us."

Julia's eyes lit up. "Fantastic," she said.

Jones gave a knowing smile. "Let me give them a ring."

Within a flash he had produced his mobile from his suit pocket and was thumbing through the address book. He resumed his pacing back and forth.

"Hey, mate," he said as the call was answered, his tone suddenly changing from gruff and weary to chirpy and familiar. "How's it all going? Yep. Yep. And the kids? How old is Kitty now? Oh really?"

Julia stared at Jones in amazement and then at Mark, who could only shrug hopelessly. For several minutes the call continued in the same vein. Whoever this contact was, Julia couldn't help feeling Jones wasn't that close to them as they seemed to have a lot of catching up to do. Years' worth by the sound of it. In exacting detail.

As Julia listened to Jones prattle on, she had to ask herself if this was really the quick option. Then again, she could remember how long it took the last time she phoned the DVLA call centre after she lost her driving licence. Maybe this wasn't so much longer than going through official channels after all.

Finally, the call seemed to be approaching a conclusion. Jones stopped pacing and brought his notebook out, leaning it on one of the bookshelves so he could write on it with his free hand. He scrawled something down. "Yep. Yep. Got it. Thanks for that, mate, appreciate it. Take care. You, too. Yeah, whenever you're next passing by let me know. Yep. Bye, chap."

He put the phone away. "Well, that's interesting," he said, gazing thoughtfully at the air.

"What is?" Julia asked.

"Kitty didn't go to university after all. We all thought she would. Such a bright kid. Learning to be an electrician instead. I always said Mark should have done a proper trade like that. He could have earned so much more."

"Dad!" Mark snapped.

Jones threw his arms out defensively. "Oh, come on, lad. It's true, don't blame me."

"No, I mean the car. What did he have to say about the car?" Mark shouted.

"All right, calm down," Jones said to his son. "He's just checking now, he'll let me know."

The two men stood scowling at one another.

"It's probably not too late to get an apprenticeship, you know," Jones said.

Mark sputtered but was saved from having to form words when his dad's phone beeped and he read a text message from the screen with a satisfied grin.

He looked up from the phone. "Mr West is the registered keeper of a 2015 white Micra automatic," he announced.

Julia rose to her feet in excitement. "Then it was him that we saw driving away from Barry's flat that day," she said.

"You fancy him for Barry's killer?" Mark asked her.

"Yes," she said. It was her turn to start pacing now, fuelled by adrenaline coursing through her veins and not knowing what to do with it. She clenched and unclenched her fists. "Yes. I think Mr West killed him."

Chapter 18

Jones's eyes swivelled left and right as he watched Julia stalking up and down.

"I still don't understand," the inspector protested. "Barry can't have killed Aimiee because he was in Ireland on the rugby tour when she went missing. What other possible reason could Mr West have for wanting to harm Barry?"

"You're right," Julia said, snapping around on her heel and facing Jones. "I don't think Barry killed Aimiee. I think Terrence did."

"Okay," Jones said, folding his arms over his chest. "So he found out that Terrence killed his daughter. Then what? He killed Terrence's brother, so that he'd know what it felt like to lose someone that you love? I'll grant you it's possible, but I can't say Mr West ever struck me as being that cold-blooded. Nor were Terrence and Barry all that close."

Julia shook her head vigorously. "No," she said. "Think about it. Mr West finds out that Terrence killed his daughter."

"How?" Mark interjected. "How would he have put it together after all this time? The building work had only just started when Barry was murdered. No one knew they were going to find Aimiee's remains in there, or that locket for that matter."

"Someone knew," Julia said.

"The killer," Jones added.

"Yes, the killer. Terrence," Julia said. "But I think there was someone else, too. Rob. Maybe he brought the air rifle from his farm. They were probably just messing about with it, but it ends with Aimiee getting hurt. Badly. And after it happens, I think they put her body in the building site for the swings, knowing it was going to get concreted over.

"But I don't think that Rob pulled the trigger. That was Terrence."

"And they both keep quiet about it all these years?" Mark asked.

"Yes," Julia said. "But when Rob sees that they're digging up the old swings, he knows what they're going to find under there. He also knows that if the police find the locket, after he claimed to barely know the girl, then it's going to look like he was the one that put her there.

"I think Rob called Aimiee's dad and I think he told him what happened the night that Aimiee died. He told him that Terrence killed his daughter."

"That much makes sense," Jones said. "But then why does Barry end up dead and not Terrence?"

"Okay," Julia said, steepling her index fingers together under her chin as she walked. "Let's say you lived out of town and you wanted to look Terrence up. Just some kid from your daughter's school so you probably don't even remember him much, if at all. How would you go about it?"

"I'd search for him in the special police database," Jones said, his voice monotone.

Julia scowled at him. "I don't mean *you*. I mean someone else. Like Mr West. How would he go about looking Terrence up?"

Jones shrugged. "He'd search for him on social media, I guess."

Julia continued. "And what social media would you use, exactly?"

"If it were actually me?" Jones said. He looked at Julia waiting for approval and she gave a nod of the head. "I'd use Facebook."

"Right, Facebook!" Julia said, glee rising in her voice. "And you're really old, Rhys. Um, no offence."

She saw the edge of his bristly grey moustache twitch. "How could I take offence at that?" he said.

"But what I mean is," Julia said, intent on pressing the argument home. "Old people use Facebook."

"Everyone uses Facebook," Jones muttered darkly.

"No, they don't," Julia said. "No one in my generation has used it in at least half a decade."

Jones looked to his son for confirmation.

"That's probably true," Mark said.

Jones sighed. "It's all WhatsSnap and InstaTok now, I suppose."

"Exactly," Julia said, and paused. "Well, not exactly. But it proves my point. It's moved on from Facebook. That's for old – I mean, your generation, Rhys."

"Mine and Graham West's," Jones mused.

"Let me check something," Julia said. She pulled her phone back out of her handbag, a quicker operation this time around, and started tapping away.

"What are you doing?" Jones asked her.

"Mmm, hang on," Julia said.

Finally she gave a triumphant squeak and showed her phone to Jones and his son. They leaned their heads in closer to look.

"Terrence's Facebook page," Mark said.

Julia tapped a finger on the screen. "And his profile photo hasn't been updated in at least five years. Probably longer." He was looking younger than when she'd seen him in his house, with a full head of hair and slightly rounder in the face.

Jones looked up and met her eye. "So you're saying that Mr West looked Terrence up and this is the profile he found?"

"Yes," Julia said. "And over the last five years Terrence has gotten older. Gotten thinner. Got a little less hair on top of his head. But his profile photo has stayed exactly the same. Just like Dorian Gray."

Jones raised an eyebrow. "That's not—"

Julia continued. "So, when Mr West finds his profile picture, it looks less like Terrence and more like—"

"His brother, Barry," Jones finished for her. She hoped there might be a low whistle of admiration for her sleuthing abilities, but there was just an asthmatic-sounding wheeze through his nose instead.

"And look there," Mark said, pointing at Julia's phone. "It still has his place of employment listed as the Barley Mow. He can't have updated this page since before he left home."

"I guess it's becoming clear what happened—" Jones began, but Julia roughly cut him off. She'd started this and she didn't intend to let the inspector swoop in just as she was finishing.

"Rob phones Mr West up," Julia said, "and tells him that Terrence killed Aimiee. Mr West then looks up Terrence's Facebook page, sees an old photo and sees he's working at the Barley Mow. So he goes to the pub and he lurks around until he sees Barry working behind the bar. He thinks it's Terrence, and at this point he leaves and waits until Barry finishes work. He follows Barry home and knocks on the door."

"Maybe Barry vaguely recognizes him from his school days," she continued. "Or maybe Mr West just talks his way in based on seeing him at the pub. Barry doesn't have any reason to be suspicious, he's honest-to-God got no idea what happened to Aimiee or that Mr West would want to hurt him. But once he's inside, he strikes." Julia mimed a stabbing motion through the air.

After finishing her speech, she looked up at Jones and Mark with satisfaction.

"I guess he realized that we saw his car leaving the scene of the crime," Mark said.

"If he didn't realize then, he would have seen on the news that the police were looking for the car," Julia said. "There were no plates but he must have thought that sooner or later he'd come up in the investigation. Especially with Aimiee's bones being exhumed so soon after."

Jones finished her thought for her. "So he drove the car back here and set it alight."

"That's right," Julia said. "Burning it here in Biddle Rhyne made us think it would be someone living locally."

Jones looked up towards the ceiling, apparently deep in thought.

"What are you waiting for?" Julia asked him. "Can't you go and arrest him?"

Before he could answer, Julia's ringtone piped up, and the sound of her and Rumpkin singing *Who Let the Dogs Out* filled the room. Julia scowled at her phone. It was Ivan ringing her, so she swiped to decline the call.

Jones didn't appear to be listening. "If Mr West does confirm that Rob messaged him, telling him that Terrence was the one who killed Aimiee, that would cast some serious doubt on Terrence's version of events. But there's still that note. His lawyer will make hay with that, no doubt about it."

Who Let the Dogs Out sounded up again.

"Sorry," Julia said, snatching her phone up. "It's Ivan. He's probably seeing if I'll work tomorrow or something. I'll tell him to go away."

She held the phone up to her ear. "Ivan, I'm really busy right now," she said.

"Yeah, okay," Ivan's voice said. "But I thought you'd want to know that Mr West just walked into the pub."

Julia went silent for a moment. "He did?"

"Yes," Ivan replied. "I asked him what car he drove but he just looked at me really oddly and now he's gone off into the beer garden."

"Keep an eye on him," Julia said. "Don't let him do anything stupid. We're on our way down."

"Good, I'm really rushed off my feet here, Julia," said Ivan.

"I don't mean to work. This is life or death, Ivan," Julia snapped.

There was a pause while Ivan weighed this. "Fine," he said.

Julia tossed the mobile back into her handbag and turned to Mark and his dad, who were staring at her expectantly. "Mr West is at the Barley Mow," she said.

"We've got to get down there," Jones said.

Mark snatched up the keys for the van from where they were lying on top of his toolbox. "I'll drive," he said.

* * *

Julia sat in the middle seat of the van, squeezed in between Mark on one side and his dad on the other. The high street sped by at an alarming rate and she clamped her eyes shut.

"Relax, Julia," the inspector said to her. "We're only doing thirty-five."

"Oh," Julia managed to force her eyes open. Somehow the urgency of the task made it seem like they were going faster. Sally normally did thirty-five down here, on the occasions that it was clear. Forty if she was late for something, or not paying attention.

They reached the end of the high street and Mark turned the van round the bend. He brought it skidding to a halt at the blue and white police barrier, still cordoning off the scene where Rob's body had been discovered that morning. Mark sat tapping his fingers on the wheel impatiently as the uniformed police constable jogged over to meet them.

Jones wound down his window and stuck his head out. He was faintly reminiscent of Rumpkin, whenever he got a chance to be in the front seat. Julia did her best to dismiss that image from her mind.

"Let us through," Jones barked as soon as the woman was within earshot. "We need to get to the Barley Mow."

The constable's eyes narrowed but she detached one end of the tape for them all the same.

"It's for work!" Jones called out to her as Mark hit the accelerator and they shot through the opening.

Julia couldn't help but steal a glance towards the passing rhyne at the spot where the body had been found. It was barely a dozen yards up from the cut-through she used. If she had been a little earlier away from work, or walked home a little faster, she might have stumbled right into Terrence as he was attacking Rob. She gave a shudder. That was an odd thought. She wondered what the outcome of that might have been. Nothing good, in all probability. She couldn't imagine she would have made much of a difference against a man of Terrence's size.

As soon as the van came to a halt, they all bundled out and hurried round to the back of the pub. Mr West was sitting alone at one of the picnic tables, gazing despondently out over the beer garden where the excavation and the mounds of soil were still surrounded by the flapping police tape. He must have noticed them coming, but he didn't look up.

As they approached, Jones pushed his jacket back, reaching for his handcuffs, but Julia pressed a restraining hand onto his arm.

"He's a dangerous man," Jones muttered to her.

"Just… give him a moment," Julia said.

Jones grunted but his hand moved away from his cuffs. "All right, but stay back, let me handle this."

Mr West sat impassively as they approached. "I thought you'd be coming," he said as they reached him. "When

Ivan asked about my car when I came in, I knew you must have worked it out."

"It's important you tell us exactly what happened," Jones said in what was for him a gentle tone.

Mr West gave out a long sigh. "I got a phone call, completely out of the blue. A man calling himself Rob. I can't say that I remembered him but he said that he'd been Aimiee's boyfriend. He said he'd taken an air rifle down to impress her, that they'd been playing around with it down there." He gestured out to the fields beyond the end of the pub garden.

"And then he said there was another boy, Terrence Long. He'd taken the gun from him. Rob claimed that the boy hadn't meant to hurt anyone, although what he expected to happen shooting an air rifle at people, I don't know. And then, since they knew the swings were being concreted over the next day, they hid her in the ground there.

"I didn't plan on killing him. I only came down to get the truth out of him. But when I saw him working here, smiling and carrying on like it was nothing when my daughter was lying right alongside him? He even joked about the swings being haunted. It was too much."

Mr West bent over and put his head in his hands, running the heels of them over his forehead. "But it wasn't even the right boy, was it?"

Jones didn't answer. In the distance the sound of sirens came from the direction of the village. Jones's back-up on their way, Julia surmised.

Mr West straightened and rubbed at his eyes. "Give me a moment to say goodbye properly, won't you?"

"Take a moment," Jones said. "Then I'll need you to come with me."

* * *

The police car pulled noisily away down the gravel of the Barley Mow's car park, bumping slightly on its suspension as it turned onto the lane and headed off towards the station at King's Barrow. Sitting in the back seat, Graham West stared straight ahead.

Hands on his hips, seemingly oblivious to the cold, Jones watched the car go. "Well," he said, his voice weary. For the first time since she'd known him, Julia thought he looked genuinely run down. "At least we have his version of events now. And a confession for Barry's murder."

"Will his version be enough to charge Terrence with murder?" Julia asked.

"Charge? Yes. Will it stick? I don't know," Jones said. "Terrence will still swear up and down that Rob killed Aimiee and then himself. The suicide note gives him a pretty strong case, at least for reasonable doubt. We might all suspect it's been forged, but we can't prove it."

The wind blew in off the moors and Julia shivered. Mark put his arm around her and the three of them stood, looking in the direction the police car had left. It was infuriating that Terrence might still get away with the worst of what he'd done. He'd killed two people. One of them he'd happily kept silent about for years while her parents fretted away. The other he had slain to keep his secret. He must have done so in cold blood, too, if he had planted that note on Rob.

So much hinged on that blasted note. Julia cursed that she'd ever spotted it. It would have been better if it had just sunk to the bottom of the rhyne, never to be seen again.

Jones turned to Julia and Mark. "I'll need you to get yourselves to the station and give your statements."

"You're not coming, too?" Mark asked.

"No," Jones said, looking up the road again. "I'm going to go and find Terrence."

Chapter 19

Julia sat in the police station with Mark at her side. They were in one of the interrogation rooms, but it certainly felt less interrogation-y than on her first visit. The chairs were just as uncomfortable and the room just as spartan, but it didn't have the same oppressive weight now she wasn't a suspect herself.

The detective taking their statements was a middle-aged woman, maybe about forty years old. She wore a painfully no-nonsense trouser suit and her greying hair was pulled back in a functional ponytail. As far as Julia could tell she was asking the same questions over and over again, each time meticulously writing their answers down in her notepad.

After some time had passed, and it certainly felt like a lot of it, the door opened and Jones let himself quietly into the room. He made eye contact with Julia and Mark, but didn't say anything. The detective interviewing them gave him a slight nod and continued her questions. Jones planted himself onto the wall behind her, arms folded across his chest.

Finally, the woman cleared her throat and gently folded her notebook shut. "I think we're all done here," she said. She seemed to look back over her shoulder at Jones for approval, but if he gave any signal in return then it was lost on Julia.

"Did you manage to bring Terrence in?" Mark asked his dad.

Jones nodded. "Yes. Picked him up at his house. He's talking to his solicitor now and then I'll see what I can get out of him."

"Is it just his word against Mr West's, then?" Julia asked.

Jones spread his hands out in front of him. "Maybe. And you placing him at the scene. Certainly nothing we have yet is definitive. It might depend on what forensics come back with. I'll see if I can turn the screw on him before then."

Julia and Mark were just standing up from the table when the door of the interrogation room opened and an older-looking constable stuck his head through the doorway.

"Suspect's ready for you, Inspector," he said, addressing Jones.

"Finally," Jones said, unpeeling himself from the wall.

"Dad, can we watch on the monitor?" Mark asked.

Before his father could reply, the other detective shot an angry glance at Mark. "That's not the way we operate here," she said sharply. "We don't just let people observe interviews willy-nilly. This is a modern constabulary and I don't know what would have given you the impression otherwise." As she stalked from the room she let her eyes linger on DI Jones, as though answering her own question.

Jones waited until the door had closed behind her. "I'm afraid I'm not a particularly modern copper," Jones admitted. "Go on, I'll sneak you in."

* * *

The TV screen was small but the picture was crystal clear. Julia and Mark watched as Jones entered the interrogation room, settled himself down across from Terrence and his solicitor, and started going through the initial formalities.

Julia didn't recognize the lawyer. It wasn't the hapless duty solicitor who had been provided to her when she'd been arrested. Even on the CCTV monitor she could tell this man was more sharply-dressed, held himself more erect and didn't have the same crushed look of despair in his eyes. Presumably Terrence's parents had managed to arrange for someone with at least a modicum of competence. She hoped Jones was up to the task.

"Let's not make this any more difficult than it needs to be," Jones said, talking directly to Terrence rather than his solicitor.

Terrence, for his part, was lounging back in his chair. He looked surprisingly smug given he'd just been arrested for two counts of murder.

Jones continued, "You've been arrested for the murder of Rob Trout. We've got a witness who places you at the scene of the crime at the time in question. Once forensics come back, I'm betting decent money that your DNA is going to be found on him.

"Would you like to save some time and confess to it now? I'm sure a judge will look more kindly on you if you do so, rather than drag this out needlessly."

Terrence's counsel gave Jones a withering look. "My client is willing to admit that he was there and that he struck Mr Trout," the man said, flattening down his already immaculate suit. "But all the evidence points to a suicide, which must have occurred after my client left the scene. As far as my client knew, Mr Trout was alive and to all intents and purposes unharmed when he left. Mr Trout's death, while tragic, was not murder."

Even on the small monitor, Julia could tell Jones was not happy with this rebuff.

"Then there's the killing of Aimiee West," Jones said, apparently ignoring what the man opposite him had said. "Before he died, Rob contacted Aimiee's father and told him that Terrence was the one responsible."

The solicitor lifted a finger into the air. "A fact which Mr Trout later recanted. In his suicide note he confessed to Aimiee's killing himself."

"It's a pity that Rob isn't here now to set the record straight." Jones scowled.

"The young man's death was tragic for many reasons," the solicitor replied. "However, it appears obvious that Mr Trout tried to pin Aimiee's death on my client and then, when conscience got the better of him, he became overwhelmed with guilt and saw fit to take his own life. I believe the note he wrote sets the record perfectly straight. And I believe a jury will agree."

* * *

Jones watched as the uniformed officer led Terrence away down the fluorescently lit corridor in the direction of the cells. He ran his fingers backwards through his matted white hair in exasperation and puffed out his cheeks.

Julia let herself collapse down into one of the padded purple chairs that lined that section of the corridor. It seemed it had been deliberately designed in order to provide the least amount of comfort possible, but she was so exhausted that she didn't care. It had been a long morning and it was catching up with her.

"Do you think he'll make bail, Dad?" Mark asked.

Jones didn't look around, although Terrence was out of sight behind the swing doors now. "I don't know," he said. "I can only hope not. At least I should be able to tie him up in paperwork for twenty-four hours while we firm our case up."

Julia pulled her bag up onto the chair next to her and looked for her phone. There were half a dozen texts from Ivan asking when she was coming in. She had been due to start her shift half an hour ago.

"I need to get to work," she said wearily, quickly thumbing a message to let Ivan know where she was.

Mark gave her shoulder a gentle squeeze. "I'll give you a lift," he said. "I assume we're done here?"

Jones nodded and Julia hauled herself up out of the chair.

"Just drop me at home, I need to change," she said to Mark as they walked towards the exit.

"I don't mind driving you to the pub," Mark said.

"I'm already late, a bit more won't make a difference," Julia said. "Besides, you'd have to go the long way to get around the police cordon. It's probably quicker if I walk and take the cut-through to the lane."

"If you're sure," Mark said as they emerged out into the bleak concrete parking area of the police station.

"Yeah, I'll be fine," Julia replied.

Chapter 20

Julia left the house and locked the door behind her, with Rumpkin happily snoring on his rug. The car was on the driveway so it seemed Sally had also realized that with the lane shut it would be quicker to walk to work.

Julia hurried as fast as she could down the string of residential streets which ran parallel to Biddle Rhyne's high street. She was already a good hour late. At least with the shop opening soon she shouldn't miss the docked wages too much. Assuming she succeeded in selling anything at all, she reflected darkly.

She knew that she shouldn't, but she made a quick detour up one of the side roads to the quiet cul-de-sac where Rob lived – or had lived, she grimly corrected herself. It was a big Victorian house built of brown stone sitting at the end of the street. It would have been quite a grand property when it was built, but decades of neglect had taken their toll and now it had cracked paint and clogged gutters. Long ago it had been divided up into flats, the bottommost of which had been Rob's.

Standing in front of it, Julia had thought she would need a cry, but actually she found herself feeling rather numb. Too much to take onboard, she supposed.

Julia shook her head and was just about to go when something caught her eye. There were some odd scuff marks on woodwork around one section of the bay window which protruded out next to the front door. With a couple of steps she crossed the narrow section of concrete that served as the front garden and took a closer look.

It was subtle, but the wood was splintered and chipped. It definitely looked like the window had been jimmied with a crowbar or something similar, perhaps a screwdriver. She gave it an experimental tug and it swung out with a creak; the latch had definitely been forced.

She frowned at it for a moment. The police had been into the place after Rob's body had been found, but she was fairly certain they hadn't clambered in through the window. She pulled her phone out and dialled Jones but it went straight to his answerphone. Next she tried the non-emergency number but all she got was an automated voice telling her there was a long waiting time and that if she needed immediate assistance she should call 999. She hung up. There wasn't any pressing danger, but according to Jones's estimate they had less than a day now before Terrence was out on the streets again.

Julia hovered on the spot for a moment in indecision. But a voice in the back of her head was telling her that if she'd dithered a little less then maybe Rob would still be alive. Who knew what Terrence might do next and who might get hurt. Julia let out a deep breath, pushed the window the rest of the way open and clambered through, stepping onto the soft carpet inside.

She quickly scanned the room where she found herself. It was a living room-cum-kitchen-cum-diner. Nothing looked out of place. Other than feeling freezing cold from the heating being off, it seemed like a perfectly ordinary room. Rob's things were strewn about the place, but in more of a lived-in, everyday mess than anything suggesting the place had been ransacked. If the place had been broken into then it wasn't clear why. The TV was still there and there was a tablet casually lying among the sofa cushions, so not a burglary.

There was a smart bang behind her that made Julia jump. She put her hand to her heart, it had just been the window swinging itself shut.

With a final glance around the room, she scurried on into the hallway. The door to Rob's bedroom was open so she made her way in. The bed itself took up most of the room. Again, nothing looked untoward. Something on the bedside table caught Julia's eye. The necklace lay there. The one stolen from Sally in the Barley Mow car park. The one Charlie had unearthed at the building site.

Julia peered down at it. It looked rather ordinary and insignificant lying there next to Rob's alarm clock. But it made sense that Rob would have fought so hard to recover it. He didn't know that the side with the engraving had come off. He would have thought if the necklace was found by Aimiee's body then it would have linked him straight to her death.

What's more, he must have been the one who stole the digger to try and take Aimiee's remains. A foolhardy effort to retrieve the necklace, bones and all.

Julia refrained from touching the necklace and turned away. There was a desk opposite the bed with a PC on it, although it was sitting at an odd angle.

Examining the desk, Julia saw that the PC had been pushed back to make room for a stack of A4 paper. This was obviously where Rob's supposed suicide note had been written. Terrence had shown a surprising attention to detail if he had broken in just to use Rob's paper, Julia thought. Unless, of course, it was somehow necessary for the forgery.

There were faint marks on the top sheet of paper. Indents from what had been written on the previous page, she realized. She held the page to the light, making out the words.

I saw Terrence kill Aimiee.

*I am so sorry I never said anything before but now I
have told Aimiee's dad.*

*I think Barry found out what his brother did and
Terrence killed him rather than let him go to the
police.*

*If I am right I fear I may be next. If this letter is
found then I guess I have been proved right.*

But in the end, maybe I got what I deserved.

Robert

Julia looked down at the paper and blinked. This was
the original note that Rob had written so carefully before
he died, naming Terrence as Aimiee's killer. And every
word in the note found by Rob's body had come from
here, but not in the same order.

She tried to piece together what had happened.
Terrence had come to Rob's home and broken in,
planning to kill him. He hadn't known that Rob had been
staying at his parents' farm. When Terrence found the note
– left there by Rob in case anything happened to him –
Terrence had set to work on a forgery. He'd taken the top
sheet off, slipped it under another of the pages scattered
on the desk, and then traced Rob's handwriting one word
at a time to create his own note.

Who knew what Terrence had done with the note Rob
wrote. If he had any sense, he would have thoroughly
destroyed it. But the indents of Rob's original writing were
still left on one of the pages he had left behind. It proved
the note found by Rob's body was a forgery.

Julia stood frozen as the realization of what she had
found was sinking in. But her thoughts were interrupted by
a soft, low creak from the other room.

Her eyes widened. That was the broken window being
opened. Was someone else in the house?

She peeked back through the bedroom doorway, through the hall into the living room, and suppressed a gasp.

Unless Barry really did have a ghost, it looked like Terrence had made bail earlier than the inspector had predicted. He was straddling the window ledge as he lowered himself into the living room.

Luckily, he was looking down watching his feet and Julia jerked herself back into the bedroom, nudging the door closed after her.

She fought down her urge to shriek and managed to still her breathing and think.

What was Terrence doing here? Possibly he had the same realization about the indents in the paper as she had, and he'd come back for it.

As these thoughts raced through Julia's head, she heard a footstep out in the hallway and then the door handle twitched.

She snatched up the sheet of paper. There was no way she was letting Terrence get his hands on that.

Desperately, she looked around. Hiding under the desk would be futile, it was the first place Terrence would be heading for. Under the bed was so packed with boxes that she'd never make space in time.

With a horrible sense of déjà vu, Julia opened the catch on the sash window, lifted it up and clambered through, landing with a bump on the patio outside. She pulled the window down after her, convinced that she saw the bedroom door start to open as she did so. She flung herself down, crouching under the window sill, listening to the sound of her own heartbeat.

Would Terrence have come back for the paper? She didn't know, but he had no reason to come looking for it in the back garden, at least. As long as she stayed quiet she should make it out of here alive.

She was dimly aware of the sounds of movement in the bedroom and she willed herself to stay still and silent, not even trusting herself to breathe.

Then, from her handbag, Julia's rendition of *Who Let the Dogs Out* rang out across the garden.

Julia scrabbled frantically for her phone and pulled it free, but she knew it was too late, she heard the thudding of footsteps crossing the bedroom towards the window.

Leaving her handbag on the ground, she set off at a sprint across the garden. The back fence wasn't too tall, only a little higher than she was. A green wheelie bin for garden waste was shoved up against it, despite the garden being bare of any foliage.

Julia jumped at the bin, failed to land and slid off onto the ground. She hauled herself up the side of it instead, stood up, wobbling for balance, and then with a slight hop managed to swing a leg over the top of the fence.

She hauled herself over the top. As she turned to drop down she noticed two things.

The first was Terrence, his body halfway out of the sash window and into the garden in pursuit.

The second was the side gate next to the house. That would have been an easier escape.

It was too late now, though, she lowered herself as gently as she could onto the ground.

She found herself on another quiet, residential street. She vaguely recognized where she was, the village was not a big place. If she got out of here and rounded the corner she would arrive on the high street, almost opposite the shop.

The paper clutched tightly in one hand, she set off at a run. She realized that *Who Let the Dogs Out* was still blaring out from her other hand. She stabbed desperately at the phone with her thumb, not daring to stop running even for a second in order to look down.

After a couple of attempts, she heard Mark's voice speaking to her. "Hi, Julia. Listen, Dad said that Terrence made bail early so I wanted to make sure you stayed safe. I'll pick you up after your shift, okay?"

"Mark!" she wailed.

"What's wrong?"

"It's Terrence," she panted. "He's after me."

Just before she reached the corner, she risked looking over her shoulder. Terrence was dropping over the side of the fence. If she was lucky, he wouldn't catch which direction she went from here.

She darted sideways, heading towards the high street.

"Where are you? Julia?" Mark sounded frantic.

Julia ignored him. "Are you at the shop?"

"Yes. Where are you?" said Mark.

"I'm coming to you," Julia said.

She heard Mark's tinny voice still talking, but she had broken into a full sprint, her phone arcing in her hand as she went. She had no idea if Terrence was still behind her, but she wasn't risking another look back, she was heading for the shop as fast as she humanly could.

With her lungs burning, she emerged onto the high street and darted straight across the road. She powered on up the stone steps of the bookshop, bursting through the front door, slamming it closed and throwing the bolt across behind her.

Panting for breath, she staggered from the entrance hall onto the shop floor where she stood gasping with her hands on her thighs.

Mark's face was the very picture of worry. "Julia," he said.

She gulped down a few more breaths. "I'm fine," she said, "I'm fine." She meant it, instantly reassured by Mark's presence. She took one more deep breath. "But, Terrence—" she managed.

"Is behind you," Mark said, looking over her shoulder.

Chapter 21

Julia gave a shriek as she turned around. She found herself face to face with Terrence. It was still unnervingly like seeing his brother's ghost. He had a humourless smirk on his pale face.

"Oh, that shriek," Terrence said, cupping his ear with his hand. "I only caught a glimpse of you in the fog. I wasn't certain I'd recognize you if I saw you. But that shriek, I recognize that for certain."

In spite of her fear, Julia felt quite affronted. She liked to think she had given a dignified call for help as she fled from him the previous day. But there were bigger and more immediate issues at hand than how composed she had been upon seeing a ghost.

"How did you get in here?" Julia demanded.

The smirk widened into a grin. "You should really get that lock fixed," he taunted her.

"It's on my list," Julia said quietly. She'd forgotten that Lance had taken a crowbar to it. At the time, it hadn't seemed as important as getting the shop floor fixed up. It did now, though.

"Call Dad," Mark said, seeing the phone still in Julia's hand.

"Oh, I wouldn't do that if I were you," Terrence said.

With that he reached under his jacket to his waistband and withdrew a long, curved kitchen knife tapering to a point which gleamed in the overhead lights. Julia didn't doubt that he would use it.

"Both of you, drop your phones on the floor and back up into the corner," Terrence ordered, jabbing the blade to direct them into the far end of the room.

Julia and Mark looked at one another, but there was nothing for it except to obey. Slowly, Julia held her hand out and let her phone drop onto the carpet.

"Move," Terrence said.

They both began pacing backwards, keeping their eyes on their captor.

Terrence walked towards them, feet moving cautiously one step at a time and keeping the knife out before him. He scooped Julia's phone up off the carpet and then retreated back beyond the door to the other side of the room.

He stopped when he reached the far wall and his eyes turned to Mark. "Where's your phone?" Terence asked.

Mark pointed across to the counter.

Terrence gave it a quick glance and seemed satisfied it was out of Mark's reach.

Julia realized it was Sally's phone, not Mark's. Thank goodness she no longer had the vibrant pink cover. She didn't know for sure where Mark's phone was but, since she'd just called him, hopefully it was in his pocket.

Terrence's gaze swivelled from one to the other. "Now, don't do anything stupid, or I'll paint the room red."

"It's already painted red," Julia snapped at him.

Terrence looked at the sheet of paper still clutched in Julia's hand.

"Throw that here," he said.

To her own surprise, Julia shook her head. "No," she said, and tightened her grip. He had killed Rob; she wasn't just going to let him get away with that.

"Now," Terrence said, taking a step towards them.

Mark laid a restraining hand on Julia's shoulder. "Let's be calm," Mark said. "We don't want to do anything we'll regret."

Terrence gave a sharp bark of laughter that echoed in the empty room. "You listen to him, Julia."

The door banged open and, as one, they all turned to look at it.

"Hello there!" Sally stamped her way into the room, a little out of breath and obviously in a hurry, her handbag held loosely in one hand and swinging as she went.

"I just realized that I left my phone in here earlier. I'd forget my head if it wasn't screwed on! Whoopsiedoodle!" she said.

She'd reached the middle of the room and now she froze suddenly, taking the scene in properly for the first time. Her gaze moved from Julia and Mark, huddled together in the far corner. She rotated slowly and jumped as she saw Terrence, who stood grimly watching her with the long blade in his hand.

"Oh," Sally said.

The knife twitched.

"Over there with the others," Terrence said.

Sally shifted her handbag so it was grasped in both hands. Whatever she kept in it looked heavy.

"Drop the bag," Terrence said.

Sally held his gaze for a moment and then the bag went tumbling to the floor.

The knife twitched again. "Move," he said.

Sally's shoulders sagged and she crossed quickly over to the corner of the room. Julia and Mark shuffled up to make space for her.

Terrence looked at the phone on the counter where Sally had been headed. "Your phone, Mark," he said.

Mark drew his mobile out of his back pocket and tossed it across the floor where it came to a halt near Julia's.

Terrence slashed the knife idly through the air in front of him, apparently weighing up the new situation.

Sally leaned her body in towards Julia, who put an arm around her, pulling her in close. "It will be okay, you'll see," Julia said.

Sally buried her head into Julia's shoulder. "Charlie's on his way," she whispered. "He wanted to lend a hand. He's bringing some of the lads with him."

Julia felt her heart flutter. Never had she been so pleased about Sally's lifelong habit of having men trail around after her.

"Well, well," Terrence said. "What shall I do with you now?"

He advanced half a step towards them when the shop door clattered open again.

Charlie strode in, in the middle of three large men that Julia recognized from the work site at the Barley Mow. They were deep in raucous conversation, guffawing laughter echoing between them.

A cheeky grin on his stubbled face, Charlie looked up with a wave. "Oh, hiya. What are you all doing over there?"

Julia's eyes bulged as she willed Charlie to look behind him, which he duly did.

The four builders turned and took in the sight of Terrence standing there, his face stony, the long knife held out before him.

"Quiet, all of you," Terrence snapped. He pointed with the knife. "Now get over there."

The four of them stood still in a block, unmoving. Charlie made a half-step advance towards Terrence, dropping his shoulder an inch as though probing for an opening, moving like a trained fighter.

Terrence brought the blade swinging through the air, catching Charlie on his exposed shoulder and cutting cleanly through coat and clothing to the flesh beneath, drawing blood.

"Ouch." Charlie recoiled backwards instinctively.

"I said, over there!" Terrence bellowed and flashed the knife again.

This time the four men went scuttling backwards, keeping their eyes on their captor.

Julia, Sally and Mark all edged up to make room, the group of them now covering the entire length of the wall. Julia, on the end, had reached the edge of the counter.

"What now?" Mark asked. "You can't kill us all."

"I reckon I could try," Terrence growled back. The stream of arrivals seemed to have unnerved him. His eyes were wild and bloodshot.

"This is daft," Charlie said. "It'd be a massacre. You couldn't take us all down."

"Want to find out?" Terrence replied.

Charlie fell silent.

Mark nudged Julia sharply under the ribs. "Hammer," he whispered.

Julia looked at him, confused. His eyes flicked quickly down to the floor behind her. "Hammer," he repeated, just as softly.

Julia followed his gaze. There, hidden away behind the counter, was his toolbox, a perfectly placed tripping hazard for the fire exit. And lying on the floor next to it was the heavy metal hammer which he could never be bothered to put away.

Their eyes met and Julia gave a subtle nod.

Mark waved his hands frantically, drawing Terrence's attention onto himself. "Come on, mate," he said, his voice high-pitched and pleading. "Have some mercy. You won't get away with it, just let us go."

"Let you go?" Terrence spluttered. "Let you go?"

When she was sure Terrence was looking at Mark, Julia reached out with one leg and carefully scooped the hammer along the floor, nudging it sliding and rolling over the carpet, until it came to rest just at Mark's heel.

Without hesitation, Mark swooped down and snatched up the hammer. He held it aloft with his arm drawn back, looking ready to strike.

Terrence looked at the hammer and his eyes twinkled with mirth. "And what are you going to do with that?" he said. "Go on, try it. I'll gut you before you even get close."

"You know," Mark said, "my dad used to coach you rugby."

Confusion flickered on Terrence's features. "What's your point?" he hissed.

"Well, my point is that I always had to go along. There was no one at home to look after me with Mum working so I had to sit on the sidelines and watch. Every Saturday morning. Rain or shine. Miserable," Mark said.

"Too much of a wuss to play, were you?" Terrence mocked.

Mark gave a half shrug, keeping the hammer raised. "Yeah, I guess so," he replied. "I was always more of a cricketer myself."

"Wimp." Terrence grinned at him. "Come on, put the hammer down, you don't have it in you."

"The thing is," Mark continued, ignoring him. "I can remember watching you play."

"And?" Terrence said.

"And," Mark replied, "I remember you were a pretty fearsome scrummager. But you could never catch to save your life."

With that Mark's hand went ratcheting forward and sent the hammer tumbling end over end through the air towards Terrence.

Terrence let out a shriek of his own and brought both hands up defensively towards his face, but the hammer went spinning over the top of them, making contact with the crown of his head with a sickening thud.

Terrence's lights went out and he fell limp to the floor, the bloodied hammer landing with a thump on the carpet beside him.

"Oh, God, is he dead?" Julia heard one of the men beside her cry.

"I don't care right now," Mark said. "Tie him up!"

Lying spreadeagled on the floor, Terrence's head jerked and he let out a low groan.

"That answers that, then," Sally murmured.

"Hurry!" Mark yelled and Julia thrust the paper towards Sally and snatched up some electrical cabling from behind the counter.

* * *

Terrence lay prone on the floor of the shop by one of the bookcases. He watched the goings-on with sullen eyes but had so far refused to speak. Several of the builders stood close-by over the top of him in case he tried anything, but he seemed subdued enough.

Eventually Julia heard the sound of an engine racing towards them and moments later Jones burst into the room. He'd already had an account of what had gone down from Mark, but he looked around, taking stock of the situation.

"Right," Jones said. "First of all, is anyone hurt?"

"No," Julia said.

"Yes," Terrence said.

"I didn't mean you; I know all about you," said Jones.

Sally draped herself across Charlie's uninjured arm and motioned towards the other. "Charlie's hurt," she said.

"It's really nothing," Charlie said.

Jones spared a quick glance at the wound on Charlie's arm. "Mark, take him to the minor injury unit, okay?"

"Okay, Dad."

With that, Jones knelt down next to Terrence and snapped his handcuffs on his wrists. "You're coming with me, my lad," he said, hoisting him back to his feet.

Julia was dismayed to see the cabling fall uselessly from Terrence's wrists as he stood.

Jones began to read Terrence his rights.

"You can't hold me," Terrence shouted over the top of the detective. "Rob killed himself, there was a note."

"You also held up a shop full of people at knifepoint," said Jones.

"I don't remember anything like that," Terrence said, but there was a murmuring of agreement from around the room.

Jones finished up reading his rights. "Like I said," he concluded, "you're coming with me."

He turned to the rest of them before he left. "My colleagues will be here in a moment to take statements," he said. As if to confirm the point, the sound of sirens rose over the gentle background of traffic. With that, Jones pushed Terrence along out of the door.

Mark watched them go, a grim but satisfied look on his face. He looked around the bookshop at the huddle of people and shook his head. "It's scary to think just how close this came to becoming a murder scene," he breathed.

Julia nodded thoughtfully. "That would have been so awful," she said. "We'd never have got the shop open in time then."

Epilogue

Julia stood with her hands on the bookshop counter and cast her eye over the shelves, each packed full of glossy, new books. It still felt slightly surreal to see it all come together after everything that had happened, and she would never forget how the community had helped repair Lance's damage.

She glanced down at the clock on her phone and stared at it until it ticked over to 9.30.

"That's it," she declared, "you can open up."

"Aye, aye," Mark said, and he turned the key in the door and pulled it open.

A small crowd flowed in from the foyer, with Sally leading the push. The group was mostly comprised of Julia's friends and family, she had to admit. Her mum was there, as well as Mark's parents. But she was buoyed to see a few other faces as well, more or less familiar from around the village. All of them had braved the cold and mizzling rain in order to see what was on offer in Biddle Rhyne's newest shop.

The crowd spread out and made a show of examining the wares on the various shelves. Julia's proprietorial instinct couldn't help but protest slightly at seeing the grubby hands pawing all over her pristine stock, but she took a deep breath and kept quiet.

Sally crossed over to the counter, leaning over it to give Julia a brief hug. "Well done," she said, before releasing her.

"Thanks," Julia replied.

"I'm sorry Charlie didn't make it," Sally said. "They're nose to the grindstone now. The forensics are all done and the council gave it their seal of approval, I don't know if you heard."

"I hadn't," Julia said. She'd been cloistered away for the last couple of days with the final preparations for throwing the doors open. If a meteor had hit Biddle Rhyne she probably would only have noticed if it had knocked books from the shelves.

She still wasn't sure what she felt about the village expanding, even if the houses weren't going up on top of what had so recently been a grave. Presumably the developers weren't putting that particular fact in their advertising brochure. At any rate, at least Ivan would be pleased. The noise of construction aside, maybe things at the Barley Mow would be a bit more placid now. Julia could look forward to visiting as a customer and spending some of her hard-earned money from the shop.

Julia saw that Sally had drifted away and was inspecting the bookshelves of the cookery section. She selected a baking book from near the top of the shelf, slid it out from its companions, and headed back towards Julia. Bless her, she must already own every baking book under the sun.

Just before Sally reached the counter, another body inserted itself in front of her. Mr Peabody stood before Julia, his expression painfully neutral. He slammed something down onto the counter. With a sinking feeling in her belly, Julia looked at what he'd placed there.

It was a thin volume entitled Health and Safety Codes in Public Life.

Mr Peabody adjusted his glasses. "I'd like to purchase this please," he said. "It will make the perfect gag gift for my colleague's retirement. It's a sort of joke, get it?"

Julia didn't get it, but she wasn't going to let that stop her ringing it up.

Mr Peabody slid a crisp ten-pound note over the counter to her and Julia slid a single penny back.

Mr Peabody plucked it up between thumb and forefinger and then stood there, bolt upright and looking expectant.

"Oh, I forgot," Julia said. She tore the receipt from the till and handed it to Mr Peabody, who folded it neatly and inserted it into his wallet.

"Thank you, Julia," he said, turning to leave.

Julia was about to take the money and put it in the till when Sally reached down and snatched it up.

"What are you doing?" Julia asked.

Sally didn't answer. She let herself around behind the till, took a drawing pin from under the counter and with great ceremony she raised the note and fixed it high up on the wall. Or at least, as high as she could reach.

"Your first sale!" Sally declared at the top of her voice.

There was a ragged cheer and scattered applause from around the shop, growing in volume, and Julia felt herself start to blush.

"Hang on, hang on," Mark said, his voice raised over the applause, bringing it to a hush. "Be careful with that note. It might be the only money we make all day."

The shop burst into laughter, and looking over the crowd of friends, family and neighbours who had come out to the launch, Julia didn't think that seemed likely.

* * *

The weeks passed and the shop's opening rush had died down. Julia didn't want to use the word 'bonanza'. Because it hadn't been one. But it had been enough to make her quietly confident about the shop all the same.

Mark loitered about the shop on a long lunch break, elbow resting on the counter. He had streaks of paint on one of his cheeks. Julia couldn't help but wonder if he'd done it on purpose to be endearing.

The door flew open, setting the bell clattering merrily, and a man walked in, briskly. He looked down at the true crime display in the window and then gave Julia a scrutinising look as he came over.

"Are you Julia Ford?" he asked. He was slightly out of breath, it seemed he'd hurried up the outside steps.

"That's right," Julia said.

"The private detective?" the man said.

Julia opened her mouth to disabuse him, but Mark answered for her before she could speak. "Yes, that's right," he said.

Julia glared daggers at Mark, but the stranger didn't seem to notice that either. "Good," he said. "Because I need your help."

Acknowledgements

As always I'd like to thank my writing group, JP Weaver, Kendall Olsen-Maier, MachineCapybara, Caitlin L. Strauss and Delilah Waan, for all of their amazing input.

And I'd like to thank again for their support my wife, my dad and especially my mum, for her help with proofreading.

Finally I'd like to thank Marianna, Erik, Polly, Annaliza, and Arianna at The Book Folks for their hard work and patience.

If you enjoyed this book, please let others know by leaving a quick review on Amazon. Also, if you spot anything untoward in the paperback, get in touch. We strive for the best quality and appreciate reader feedback.

editor@thebookfolks.com

www.thebookfolks.com

More fiction in this series

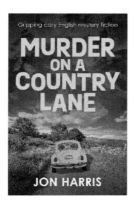

MURDER ON A COUNTRY LANE (Book 1)

After the shock of discovering a murder victim, young barmaid Julia isn't too perturbed because local garden centre owner Audrey White was a horrible so-and-so. But when her fingerprints are found all over a death threat, Julia becomes the police's prime suspect. Equipped with an unfetching ankle tag she must solve the crime to prove her innocence.

FREE with Kindle Unlimited and available in paperback!

Other titles of interest

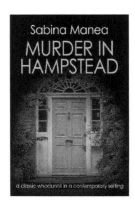

MURDER IN HAMPSTEAD
by Sabina Manea

After ex-lawyer, now interior designer, Lucia Steer accepts a job renovating a large London house, she has no idea she'll discover the owner dead. Lucia is determined to unlock the secret of this closed room mystery, no matter the trouble she'll inevitably land in.

FREE with Kindle Unlimited and available in paperback!

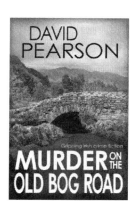

MURDER ON THE OLD BOG ROAD
by David Pearson

A woman is found in a ditch, murdered. As the list of suspects grows, an Irish town's dirty secrets are exposed. Detective Inspector Mick Hays and DS Maureen Lyons are called in to investigate. But getting the locals to even speak to the police will take some doing. Will they find the killer in their midst?

FREE with Kindle Unlimited and available in paperback!

Sign up to our mailing list to find out about new releases and special offers!

www.thebookfolks.com

Printed in Great Britain
by Amazon

When an amateur sleuth's pub colleague is bumped off, can she work out who called time at the bar?

Since getting her life back on track after bein wrongly accused of murder, Julia Ford is finall realizing her ambition of opening a bookshop the sleepy English village of Biddle Rhyne.

But, best laid plans and all that, things go awr when she stumbles upon the body of Barry, wh worked alongside her in the local pub.

That another murder has occurred doesn't take much deducing: the knife sticking out of h back strongly suggests it was no accident.

This is just the beginning of a series of strange occurrences including stolen diggers, giant haystacks, haunted playground swings, and human remains that drag Julia, kicking and screaming, into another serious(ish) investigatior

Juggling a nascent career in crime-solving with one bookselling, Julia has a lot on her plate. Can she ca another killer, or was her first case beginner's luck?

MURDER IN A SOMERSET VILLAGE is the second book in a series of humorous mysteries set in the West Country.

THE BOOK FOLKS
www.thebookfolks.com

ISBN 9781804621301

9 781804 621301

9 0 0